Jesse & Elvis

Vere McCarty

Jesse & Elvis

Fast Books

FAST BOOKS
P.O. Box 1268
Silverton, OR 97381
fastbookspress.com
info@fastbookspress.com

Set in Bodoni Book
Book designed by John Labovitz

ISBN 978-0-9794736-1-6

Dedicated to all of us who are recovering from
all sorts of things and
trying to get on with our lives.

~MILLY, HAND MAMA THE SCISSORS. Milly was sitting on the windowsill in her cotton dress with a tee shirt underneath to keep out the cold, her patent leather heels drumming against the wall.

~ Millicent? Milly slid down, hop-scotched over the clothes strewn on the floor, peered tip-toe over the ironing board and found the shiny scissors.

~ Come up here and cut this for mama.

Milly climbed up over wadded sheets. The baby lay between the lady's fish-white veiny legs that were always covered by a dress except when a baby is born. A long wet lacy thing came out of the baby's slack little tummy and ran in a loop over miss Gladys's belly that was still big and lumpy and went into her dark squishy place that seemed to breathe in and out. It looked like a wet soda straw between her mama's bloody-watery fingers.

~ Hurry now baby. Cut it. Jus like you cut mama's thread.

Milly got her little hands to open and close the scissors.

~ Good. Get down now, stay out the way.

Milly crawled backwards off the bed. Her mama lifted up the baby by its heel. ~ Ohhh. Pitiful little thang. She laid it down right on top of the scissors. But it didn't cry. It was all bluish and greenish and had a purplish swollen thing that meant it was going to be a boy.

~ Holy Lord! the lady was hollering. Have mercy Jesus!

~ Let go my arm miss Gladys. Crise amighty you make such a rumpus.

Her legs thrashed and tangled in the sheets. The midwife risked getting kicked to peer in and see what was wrong. ~ Another one coming, miss Gladys. You got ta hold on.

~ Jesus Jesus Jesus!

~ Thas right, the Lahd gonna help you now. Milly, you go on…

Milly had her palms on the sill, her butt against the wallpaper, ready to hunch back up on the windowsill, when she heard her mama's tone change. ~ Go on an get missis Presley.

~ Yes mama. But first she went to the bed and reached over with both hands and took the baby's head and pulled him out from under the lady's shiny fat knee and swung him down and laid him in her doll basket and covered him up with her doll blanket. She felt her mama's knuckles on her back.

~ Yes mama. Picking up the straw basket with both hands, she lugged it to the bedroom door and turned around to see her old dolly on the sill looking across the dirty window where streaks of rain were hitting and her mama bending over the screaming miss Gladys.

The front room was pungent with stale beer and full ashtrays. ~ Jesus take me! Take me home! Then it was quiet. Milly turned the knob with both hands and went out on the rickety porch, and here came missis Presley, bothered by the wind, with a big basket on one elbow. She gave Milly a plastic flower smile, ~ What do you have there, Millicent?

~ Baby Jezuz.

~ Can I see?

~ He sleepin.

~ Well then, we had better not disturb him. Huffing up the steps she let go of her scarf to touch the rubber bands in Milly's hair. ~ How is the mother doing?

~ She making a big rumpus, missis Prezley.

The lady peered down with the disapproving look Milly always got when she answered questions.

A pickup came by on the lane, slowed almost to a stop and then kept going. Rain sliced through the dust, making the smell of mud. Milly tried not to bump the baby with her knees. There was the pickup setting still with smoke puffing out the back and mister Vernon sticking his big orange head out the rolled-down window. The woman he was talking to held her magazine over her head, and in that pose, if you wanted, you could see the touch of mulatto in her. Mister Vernon tapped his cigarette hand like he was hearing blues in his head. But then the man and the woman both turned their heads to a new sound, a young wail that came down the lane all the way from miss Gladys's bed.

Milly went into her own yard and under the slow rain drumming on the porch roof and shoved the door open with her little hip. She felt all grown up, coming home worn out like this, and ran the back of her arm over her brow. She knew where her old basinette was and dragged it out from under the bed and dumped out her old baby clothes and set it on a chair. She took a pan from the stove and went out to the pump and critched the handle up high and hung all her weight on it to swing it back down. With the third trip down here came the gurgly gush and the rising tune of water in the pan.

She still didn't know how to load the firebox. She had tried it once and only got smoke. But this morning her mama had put in the paper and kindling and was just about to strike the match when she got called away. Milly struck the match and lit the paper and pulled her hand out when the flame flared up. She lifted up the pan, shivering as water splashed and ran down her arms and shshd on the black stovetop. She put in more pitchy pine and it started popping. She scrutched the other chair over and climbed up and dipped her fingers in the water every few moments. Finally it was comfy and she took the warm black handle with both hands, her arms shaking with the wobbling weight, and poured it splashing into the basinette. She picked up the baby, all floppy and blue, and sat him in the bath. He slid down till his little chicken neck was wet. ~ Do you like this, baby Jezuz? He did. He wiggled the tiny little fists of his feet and blew bubbles out his little flat nose. She trickled water over his head, melting the lardy stuff that was on it and he liked that too. After a while the water stopped steaming and he started puckering his face.

The door scooched open and her mama backed in, set down her bag, unloaded a big sigh and ran the back of her arm over her forehead. She was hovered over the love seat about to plunk down, when her nostrils caught the pitchy smoke and she spied the red firebox. ~ Millicent! You gon burn the house down. That was when she saw the baby's face, like a sad little old man, sticking out of the bath water. Her fingers spread like a stain over her heart, which was so discom-bobulated she could not even shriek.

~ Drink your milk now, baby Jezuz. The baby lay across Milly's lap and drank from her old bottle. He was almost a day old, and he never had cried yet, not even a peep.

~ Even if he was yours, said her mother, you couldn't call him Jesus.

Milly didn't look up.

~ Jesus is a set-aside name, jus for the son a God.

A tapping of a wedding ring on the door pane made

them both jump. Milly popped up, dropping her infant on her shoe tops with a little clunk. ~ Mwa, he said, like he was disgusted with her. Her mother threw a dish towel over him and searched frantically for a place to hide a baby in a leaky one-room frame house.

~ It's missiz Prezley, mama.

~ Better let her in, baby.

Milly turned the knob and Minerva Presley stuck her head in. ~ I found your baby, Millicent.

Milly supported herself with the doorknob.

Missis Presley smiled from one edge of her scarf to the other. ~ Aren't you going to let us in?

~ Let missiz Prezley in, Millicent.

The woman crossed the threshold, with that air of victory some people get when they feel themselves welcome in your house. ~ Your baby looked so lonesome that I just had to bring her over to you. She put her basket on the floor and bent uncomfortably and brought out the rag doll, supporting its head so that its neck wouldn't flop.

~ Don't want her no more, said Milly.

Missis Presley suddenly looked like her feet hurt. Milly got a look from her mother like she had poked somebody's eye out. ~ Sorry missiz Prezley, said Milly, and held out her arms for her old dolly.

~ Here Miz Minnie, sit down. I was just going to make tea.

~ Why thank you Edna. I need to be going, but… She waved her behind in the air.

Milly snuggled the doll baby close, over where some milk had dribbled on her shirt. The lady was looking sweetly at her while her mother picked up the wet diaper and wrapped it in a towel, and used the towel to wipe the flour from her hands, and stuck it under her arm and turned the chair sideways at the table for the lady to set her soft bottom on. ~And how is your granchild doing, miz Minnie?

That was the right question, or close enough, and the lady flew into it. ~Gladys is going to spoil that boy just like my son spoils her. He does everything for her. Goes to the store for her, reads her the paper, opens cans, everything. She has no diss-ipline. She holds the boy all the time, hasn't put him down yet since he was born. She ran out of bress milk and sent Vernon to the store for formula. Imagine.

Milly leaned against the cool tin of the flour bin, rocking her doll baby to the lady's satisfaction. She put its little stuffed face to one of the two little bumps under her tee-shirt, but quit that before the lady looked at her, calculating that she would find some bad in it.

~Her mother was like that. Forever fussing over some-body. The lady took out a cigarette and tapped it on the tabletop and held it like a piece of chalk. The water chummed on the stovetop and quieted in a cloud of steam while the hostess looked for matches. Milly pointed her eyes under the stove and her mother saw and picked them up and rattled the box.

~Water's ready Edna, said the lady, puckering up for a light. She held her breath and smoke dribbled out her nose. Her ears perked up to a faint noise from the flour bin. Her feet raised up on their toes under her. She pulled her hem farther down over her knees with one hand. She balanced her cigarette with lipstick already on it on the Missippi state ashtray and picked up the teaspoon with her finger and thumb and jingled her two lumps of sugar. She searched with her heels for a chair rung, and sat all raised up on her tailbone and her pointy toes, her perfume swamping the room.

~ Is your tea warm enough miss Minnie? ...What's the baby's name?

~ Elvis.

~ Alvin?

~ Elvis. That was my uncle.

~ That's a nice name.

The lady took a sip and relaxed a little. ~We were going to name him Jesse after my father. But Jesse Presley...? Gladys wanted to name him Tom.

~ He's a lively one. Strong enough for two.

Milly knew this was a test as soon as she got that now-you-keep-still-or-else look from her mother.

The lady said, ~ I have a pitcher back from the drug store. Bending to fiddle in her basket she made a peep of air like when you tie a balloon, and coughed.

Edna pulled the string on the light bulb that dangled from the ceiling. ~ I'm going to get a shade for this, she said.

~ Oh, that reminds me. The lady put her hand in her dress pocket and came out with a green and greasy-gray bill, with fives appearing in the corners under the jiggling light.

~ Bless you missiz Prezley, but you don't have to…

~ No, no Edna. A laborer is worthy of her hire. The lady's air of triumph was back, and she picked up her basket and held it to her as she stood up.

A pickup door slammed outside, confirming the sound of tires Milly had heard pulling up on the puddly street. She left her dolly sitting up against the flour bin and skipped over to open the door for mister Vernon. His saddle shoes creaked and he stepped in like it was nothing to come into somebody's house, except that he bent a little sideways, like his mama had hold of his ear. He said, ~ Hello Edna. And, ~ Hello Milly. There was rain in his hair and yellowish whiskers on his neck and he smelled like his living room, except sour from the rain. He had to go back out to the pickup to get an umbrella to hold open for his mama until the wind blew it inside out.

Milly held her breath until she'd heard two doors bang and the engine rev and the tires pull away through the puddles. Then she and her mother ran to the flour bin and tipped it open. The baby was blowing white bubbles out his nose, his little purple lips lavender with the flour, his face white as a ghost.

Throughout Jesse's childhood it always seemed like something was going to happen. His eyes did turn brown, well at least hazelly greenish brown, and he grew into a soft thin boy with big feet. They frizzed his hair and kept him in, and his skin went powder bluish like a sickly colored child. When he was seven-and-a-half they put him in school with his auntie Milly. The principal said he could pass for white if he weren't so slowly.

One Sunday when Jesse was thirteen he went out during the sermon for a smoke. A white boy with silky dirty-blond hair was sitting there on a pile of broken concrete, smiling into the dim fall sun. Seeing Jesse's matches blowing out he got up and walked over, his suit trousers bobbing on knotted suspenders. ~ My daddy rolls his own. Says they don't kill you as quick. He cupped his hands around the flare and Jesse pulled in the flame and handed it to him. The boy took it between two fingers and the end lit up orange and he puffed his cheeks and coughed out a cloud of smoke.

~ Shee, said Jesse. You a virgin?

The boy laughed and coughed some more. Pimples stuck out of his forehead, like Jesse's forehead. His face was kind of crooked, his nose a little flat. He handed the cigarette back. The tip was wet.

~ Shee, said Jesse. What you doing down here?

~ Nothin, the boy shrugged. Name is Elvis.

~ What kind a name is that?

The boy shrugged again with a crooked grin. Jesse

hung the cigarette between his lips and put out his hand.
~ Jess Martin.

The boys shook hands soft and quick, this year's
handshake, forty-eight. Elvis took another puff. A rumble
traveled through the church frame, people standing up.
The boy leapt up the steps of the little porch and cracked
the door open.

Here came the piano, *Rum dum dum ti ti ti ti ti ti...*
and you already knew the song.

> H-woi shud a-i fee-eel diss-cahrige
> en wo-ai shiud the sha-aa-lows co-ome?
> *Tli ti ti ti twi?*

The boy's ear was pinned to the crack in the door.
~ Big sista Rose, Jesse said to his other ear. Knock down
the walls a Jerryco, jus her voice.

> Whoi shood my heah-rt fee-eel lonely
> a-an loh-oh-ong fa heaeh-vu-u-u-un an
> ho-oh-oh-ome?

~ Don' do nothin but sing and eat. Eat like a convic.
God got to see her ever time he look down. Ought to see
her sweat too. Bucket loads. Packs this big ol hanky
between her bress.

> Hh-wen Jee-suhs i-iz my o-shun
> an my cohn-stun f-ri-i-i-n iza hee-ee-e-e
> you know his oaai iz own the lidlol spair-row
> an ai kno-o-ow he ca-e-ahs fa yoo-n mee.

When sister Rose's voice slid down the word sparrow,
the boy's fuzzy adam's apple did the same, the corner of his

mouth jumping like his cheekbone had it on a string.

…*Rum ta ti.* The pastor's voice spoke, ~Yes I know he is watching me. Halleluia. The soft swoosh and rumble of people sitting down.

The boy swung himself down over the two-by-four banister, to where Jesse was sheltering a fresh cigarette against the white-painted plywood wall. The boy said, ~ I'm moving to Memphis. That's why I come over today.

Jesse handed it over. ~You ought to come winsdy nights. Sangin's better.

The boy kept it dry this time and didn't cough. ~ I'm moving today.

~Today? Memphis? You lyin.

The corner of the boy's mouth went up. ~They're all loaded up. My ma probly cryin, thinkin I changed my mind and don't want to go. Daddy's sayin, Naw, he'll show up. He don't want to miss Memphis.

~What you going to do in Mempfis?

~ Play git-tar. You ought to come up. They got skittle up there, an race music, an everything.

~We never go nowhere. They hardly never let me leave the house.

~ My ma is like that too. My daddy don't care though.

Jesse frowned. ~My daddy don' care neither. Sure you ain't lyin?

The door opened and darkened, and the porch creaked under the pastor's shined shoes. He scratched under his belly and fished out his pipe and match sticks. Jesse's cigarette fell to the ground behind his back and his heel found it on the first try.

~Ain't you at the wrong church son?

~I already been to church sir. Come over to hear the music.

Pastor sipped at his pipe and said, ~We worship the Lahd through the music.

Jesse leaned against the wall and watched this new boy charm the old man right out of his suspenders.

~Yes sir. I come to worship too. The music is worship-ful. That's why I like to come over here.

~Next time, come right in the front door, heyuh?

~Yes sir.

~Brother Gains your pastor?

~Yessir. He says good things about you.

~He know you're here?

~No sir. But...

The man tapped his pipe on the railing. ~Vehra good. Give brother Gains my regahds.

~See? said Jesse when the door shut. You lyin.

The boy shrugged and gave his hand again and zig-zagged out through the mess the bulldozer had made of the back lot. You could see him singing, and hear little pieces of his voice.

Jesse took out three cigarettes and put two in his shirt pocket and one back into the pack. His mama would be going downstairs to serve dinner. He met up with his auntie Milly on her way home. She was skinny except for her butt and it was hard to keep up with her.

~ Here Mimi. He handed her the crinkled pack.

~ Dam, Jesse. I told you not to smoke em all. You're going to get a heart attack. She hardly slowed her walk as she flicked her lighter and lit up.

~ What about you.

~ What bout me what.

~ You smoke more'n me.

She talked exhaling, ~ Who gives a care about me. Quit scuffling your feet.

~ Shee. Mill? How long we have to stay in Tupelo?

When he had said that she actually looked at him. ~ Leave your face be, baby. You'll get pock marks.

When Jesse looked old enough he signed up for a hitch in the army and went overseas, where he was shot in the boot and bled in the wet snow, and spent the rest of his time in Fort Bragg, which was like a zero-security jail in a beach town in a foreign country. They put him on KP and he peeled potatoes and cooked the army way. Out of boredom he experimented with the white watery potatoes that sprang up from the dune soil. He tasted the mild paprikas you could get in the City, and tried using pink Hawaiian sea salt to brighten the yellow from Korean cooking oil. He made different cuts and cooked them at different heats and tried them out on pretty much everybody. He had a hit on his hands, and in deference to those who thought of him as a lazy southern boy, which was pretty much everybody, he called them suthren frazz.

When his hitch was up he got a ride to Mendocino with a second lewey. In his waxed DeSoto, over It's cherry pink, and apple blossom white... mewing on the radio, the guy wanted to talk what-are-you-going-to-do-with-your-life.

~ Gonna go to music school, said Jesse.

~ That's bitchin but you need to do something practical too.

~ Yeah, I'd like to run a restaurant, or maybe a hotel.

~ Well, you got the talent. Tell you the truth, I kind of envy you. You got your whole life ahead of you.

Jesse went walking on the beach, his army shoes laced over his shoulder. He listened to the waves build and break and roll and run up to his bare feet and stay still for an instant and drag back again and mosh into the water spilling from another wave. The wet sand and salt soothed his feet at first but then it got into his wound. He bought one of those see-the-country bus tickets. The first bus was going to Arizona. Waking up one afternoon he saw a shoe store with a Big Sale banner. He got down off the bus, stowed his bag behind the counter in the station, and walked back up Camelback Road. He wished he was carrying something to disguise his limp. In the lot between the shoe store and an Indian jewelry shop hunkered one of those permanently-parked square vans with the side cut out, leaking a cloud of steam with an aroma of onions and chili. Inside that aroma a boy straddled his bicycle, The Sun in red paint letters on the canvas bag half full of newspapers on his handlebars. Gene Krupa drummed on the radio. A man appeared in the slid-back window, a week's whiskers on his face. ~ Chili and onions?

~ Yes please, the boy said.

In his hand the man balanced a bun with a generous hamburger, ladled the chili, paused to ask, ~ You like mustard too?

~ Yes sir.

He squoze the mustard on, folded wax paper around it. ~ Sure you aint spoiling your supper? The boy didn't answer, gave him four bits and got change back.

While Jesse waited he noticed a little sign taped to the mixer, For Sale $~~1200~~ 1000. He ordered his chili burger and asked for change for the telephone.

~ Where ya calling to?

~ Mizzippi.

With a pile of coins in his hand the man complained, ~ I aint no piggy bank, ya know.

Jesse pulled out another bill and said, ~ Let me try your fries. Although he knew by the smell they wouldn't be as good as his.

It was three in the afternoon. That would make it five or six back home. ~ Milly?

~ Jesse. They let you out?

~ Yeah. Listen Meem, how much money you got?

~ Not much. You in trouble baby?

~ Naw. I want to buy a… kind of a restaurant.

~ A what?

~ Okay, a hamburger stand.

~ Ahuh. How much you need.

~ Four, five hunerd.

~ Humh. Mama got some money. She over at the pas-sor's house right now.

~ Shee.

Jesse had made the down payment and was simmering chili and chopping onions when Milly pulled up in a taxi cab. He gave the cabby a chili dog for a tip. He pulled his hamburger man hat down over his bad haircut and showed Milly how to make shakes and pour sodas.

~ I know how to make a shake, baby. Put that milk away.

~ Well, try these fries.

Behind the van was a trailer house. You just went down out of what used to be the passenger door of the van and up in the trailer door. Milly paid the rest of the money. The man said, ~ 'Sall yours. Sorry I didn't clean it up better. I left the TV for ya. He drove away in his Nash with his dog looking back over the fishing poles bent across the rear window.

Cleaning up the place they turned up the radio, bundled up newspapers, swept dead flies off the sills, washed bedspreads in a mayo bucket. Milly stood below the back door, her cotton dress flapping in the night wind, pulling out handfuls of dog hair from the hoover bag. ~ Ought to put an ad on that station.

...I don't know what you call this nex tune, I jest know I dig it. This goes out from Arlene to her luva main, an from yors truly to you cats out cruisin tonight, an also to Nizhoni from Chris away out there in San Carlos, an I hope we're comin in loud an clear cause this nex tune is sumpin else.

A rockabilly strum over the AM, the guitar not quite grooving with the bass. ...Well ats alright mmama, aats alrigh fa yeou... The voice was quavery, scratchy and eager.

Jesse stood in his tracks. ~ That aint Arthur Crudup?

~ No baby. Don't you know who that is?

A little electric decoration and the song sat down. ... Weh mama she done tol me...

~ Sure I know the song, but the voice is way outa control.

J ESSE AND MILLY WERE REMODELING the shoe store when It's Now or Never hit the hit parade. The Return to Sender LP was getting its scratches by the time they backed in a flat-bed and unloaded the big gas grill. They sponsored little league and joined the church choir. They stocked the juke box with old Elvis records, Ray Price and BB, and Jimi and Janis, and then Aretha and new Elvis records. And over in J and K they kept some Sun records with Carl Perkins and some Willa Mae Thornton and Junior Parker and what-not. Milly made scrapbooks, mixing in magazine pictures with snapshots of their lives – a trip to the Grand Canyon, Elvis in the army, a pow-wow at Gila River, the happily repressed couple Elvis and Priscilla and their baby, a magazine picture of Graceland next to a photo of their new Burger Joint sign. The neighborhood grew and so did business, and a generation of migrants from everywhere else had their sock hops and car washes and Rotary meetings and their burgers and frazz and root beers after games and felt at home at the Joint.

Milly was making two malts, one chocolate and one

vanilla, and she almost missed the question because of the whizzz of the beaters. The deejay was saying, … Ahright Elvis fans, an lets just admit it, we're all Elvis fans. Right here in front of me I got a pair of, are you ready for this? a pair of Tower of Power tickets to the big concert coming up Friday night. They're all yours if you can answer one question. Ready Elvis fans? Here we go. Most people think Elvis was an only child. But actually Elvis had a brother, make that a twin brother, who died when Elvis was born. Kind of sad when you think about it. That was in nine-teen-an-thirty-five, can you picture that, forty-two years ago. Yes, believe it or else, Elvis is over forty. Okay that was the intro. Now for your Tower of Power question.

The phone rang on the radio. …What was the name of Elvis's brother who died at birth? Tower of Power fourteen-ninety you're on the air.

Hello?

Hello caller, you're on the air. What was the name of Elvis's twin brother?

Oh. Elvis's twin brother?

Right. Take a guess.

Oh. Alvin?

Great guess. But no cigar. Thank you for tuning in to the Tower. Four-oh-nine one-four-nine-oh, let's take another caller, two fabulous tickets to the big Tower of Power concert. Come in caller you're on the air.

Uh yeah. Oh hey I love your show.

Thank you. Got any idea what…

I read a book about this. Was it Red? Or Buddy?

 …*Tan-tan tan-tan tan-tan tan-tan Tan!*

~ No, and no. Thanks anyway and thanks for tuning in.

 …Uh baby led mih be, y luhvin teddy beyh…

Milly poured the malts and put them on a tray. The phone rang and she took an order, while Carly hollered in through the window, ~ Two cows one pink, one barley brown and lumpy.

Milly wiped her fingers on her apron. With the Jordanaires doing …Hopadahda hopadahda…, and Elvis coming in with …Oh wonzhaledme be… she picked up the phone and dialed. Busy signal. She put the lids on a strawberry shake and a chocolate malt, rinsed off the beaters and dialed again. Busy.

The next caller was hopeful. Was his name Teddy?

Aaron Presley, said the next, sounding very sure.

As she dialed again the deejay was sounding irritated. No, it wasn't Elvin. Great guess though. Tower of Power you're on the air.

~ His name was Jesus, but they call him Jesse. Milly heard her voice kind of vibrate.

Did you say Jesse? Caller, did I hear you say Jesse?

~ Yes I did.

Jesse turned and looked at her. With her palm over the phone she said, ~ We won the tickets baby.

~ Tell im your name.

~ Oh. This Milly Martin.

Milly? Milly at the Burger Joint?

~ Ats right.

Hey Milly, you gon be open at ten?

~ We closin at ten but...

~ Tell em we'll stay open Meem.

~ We be here.

Can you have some suthren frazz waitin?

~ You got it.

Milly, you like Ray Chawls?

~ Thas ma main man.

The main man's distinctive left hand started up.

~ Pink an brown up!

~ What you say?

~ Jesse man, we're outa straws. Three frazz jumbo make it four got it Mills?

~ What you think?

The Stamps had been stretching their material for a while when Milly and Jesse arrived. The armory was packed, people standing behind the added card chairs. Bic lighters twinkled around the arena. Milly led Jesse blind-walking down the middle aisle, into a traffic jam where the ushers waved their pen lights hunting for the source of a wafting hit of hash. Folks were talking out loud, and the sound man turned it up and the talking got louder. Milly and Jesse took their seats just as the Oooh commenced of He Touched Me. They kept the crowd for a verse and a chorus, but lost them again and the lead guy glanced toward the wing, messing up his lyrics…. I shouded while mmm… eternidy… They finished the song and walked off like they'd been relieved from duty in Nam. A lull. Scattered laughter. We want the-king. We want the-king. Elvis's drummer came out, sticks in hand, and tuned up his drums and the crowd was impressed enough to shut up for a minute. The guitar players won applause for the way they threw their straps over their shoulders. Two of the Sweet Inspirations, looking sleep-deprived under their afros, got used to the stage while the crew fussed with the mikes. Now they stepped and swayed and the Stamps, in dowdy checked jackets, took their places at the side. They all looked at each other, afraid to commit to a crescendo. The crowd stomped, We. want. the-King. We. want… Cheers erupted and there he was, a blob in a spangled white jumpsuit slo-moing himself to center stage and taking the mike in his fat ringed hand. A kind of shock set in. Just a whistle and a whoop from the corners of the crowd.

~Ah shankoo. Shankoo vera mush.

This self-satire raised hopes.

~Puut your hand in the hand of the man… It was Elvis somewhere down in the throated words, nowhere near the notes. The backup singers came in strong, … Stilled the water…

They got through the number, closing it with… The man from a-Ga-a-luh-leee… stretched way out, the bass singer sliding way way down. The Inspirations no longer swayed much, but held hands tightly, the taller one with silvery-blue mascara running down her high brown cheeks.

To make up for almost not starting at all, the applause was extra loud. ~ Fuckit, said Elvis under the noise. Ah'm dyin. But then, as the applause got confused, he sweet-talked, Well, we're here, in spite of what you may have heard. His doughy cheeks dimpled and he made a smirk toward his trio and they were laughing ahead of cue. ~ This is what we a-love to do. At leas it pays the tax man. Come on JD, swing us down.

The singers rocked right into it. Suhhh-wing down charriot stopan let me ride, suh-wing… They backed off and let Elvis's voice be heard when he was on key. Under the boofed-up hair and jet-set shades it was still Elvis with his smirky lip and music dribbling unevenly from his soul. That was the slippery thing the crowd tried to hold onto.

Elvis went to the piano and the camera man rolled in close and things went better. Except that he forgot about the crowd and played just for himself. His voice was a half-controlled quaver. ~ I am tard an ah need… ma strenth an par…

Milly said, ~ Z'like going to a funeral. Jesse didn't answer. Holding onto his arm she felt him shaking.

~ …Justa open, my aa-aais, that a-aai might se-ee-

ee-hee... The place felt very still. In the glow of lighters tears glistened on lots of faces.

Elvis left the piano and wobbled to the mike, and it happened somewhere in All My Trials. He bent over. He kept the mike under his chin and pretended it was from emotion, but from the front rows you could see the pain. The band teetered on the edge of panic. ~ Only one thang that money can't buy, Elvis mouthed, ... true love that will never die... truer words never spoken and all my trials, Lord... soon... fuh... gotten. The crowd was weeping openly when he blew kisses and walked away. The Sweet Inspirations went into a tight dance so that you wouldn't look at the fat ass and the knock-kneed waddle. The band filled in with a gospel tune, then another.

A tall man in a bad suit came on stage. The band stopped. Aylvis tole me to tale you, he began. Aylvis tole me ta tale you all thet he loves ya. Do yall love Aylvis? Let em know it. Let em heyah ya back stage. Ah rat. Ah rat. Ah... Ah rat heyahs wut we gon do. Ya got ya teekit stubs? Holem up, lehme see um. Ah rat. Hole ondo um. Hole ondo um coz come winsdy nat ogus sivinteenth, we gon come back heeayh. Owuh boy gonna git well in this good Airizona eyah, an he gon rock this place. Yall got the kah-nol's gah-ron-tee own that.

Sometimes you can't see the sky, even in Desert City.

A high fog hangs over, catching the rising dust and smoke, smudging the smaller stars and making it look like the whole sky was just a few blotchy big stars. Then, as if the neon bouncing off that lid was not enough, you have streetlights going up everywhere, as in this parking lot.

Jesse reached in the window of the Studebaker and opened the door for Milly. She got in and cranked the engine. She tried again. He opened the hood. It chugged over slower. He lifted the carburetor cover. When he straightened up he saw someone big, a gone-to-seed middle-aged man, shuffling toward them.

~ Fifty-two Baker?

~ Fifty-four. Piece a junk.

The man wore a cheap blue bathrobe half-open over orange pajamas that shimmered under the lights. He took off his sunglasses and looked into the darkness that smelled of burnt oil. ~ What's the plan?

~ Prime it I guess, said Milly.

Jesse took out his Winstons, tapped the pack and offered one. ~ Don't smoke, said the man. Only thang I never do. He tried to laugh, but was too tired.

Jesse laughed for him. Milly brought the gas can. Jesse shook it. ~ Fumes.

Taking out her Kools Milly said, ~ You who I think you are?

The man struck a lame karate pose, then let it go. ~ Yeah, it's me. You caught the show?

Milly took a puff. Fussing with the carburetor Jesse

said, ~ Guess you could call it that.

Elvis leaned in with him. Jesse handed him the air filter and wiped his hands on an oil rag. ~ What's with the duds?

~ They checked me into the hospital. All doped up and still can't sleep. Cops are out looking for me right now. Ol story.

~ Shees.

Out of the lit-up night a pop and hum, fifty-seven chevy, red and white paint just made for these lights, prowled over and sat there thrumming, the radio leaking ...Toonaaeetz the noit, it's gwonna be oll roiit... like a cloud of helium. Two young slicks jumped out.

~ Hah! Elvis stepped into the dragon position, his rings catching the light.

~ Whoa pops. Don't hurt yself.

~ You ain't... No. Man, I heard you stank it up tonight.

~ Thas all right, said Jesse. Wer all friends. Got any gas Del?

~ You run outa gas Hamburg? No way.

~ It's his carb. Candi, throw me the keys.

The muffler roared and went silent along with the radio. The girl jingled the keys out the window. Del popped the lid and rummaged in the trunk. ~ Where's the dam gas can? Screw it, this'll work. He brought out a loop of plastic tube. Don't tell me you got a safety on this piece a...

~ Naw. It'll go down.

It did, and Del leaned over the rear of the dull-painted Studebaker and mouthed the tube and in a moment gas was tinkling into the pop bottle Milly was holding.

~ Fuzz, said Del.

Candi patted the upholstery and said, ~ In here, Elvis. Whoa, I can't believe it. Come in here with me. Del put the siphon tube in his hand and pushed him toward the open car door.

The black and white Fury pulled up, engine throbbing, and a cop leaned his square brown head out. ~ What's goin on?

~ Hamburger's old wreck is broke down again.

~ Oh. You need help Jess?

Jesse shook his head, as the cop looked everybody up and down.

Del said, ~ We got it covered, Jimmy. I mean officer Jenson.

The cop frowned. ~ Hey by the way, you men seen anything unusual tonight?

~ Like what.

~ Like anybody unusual?

~ What, around here?

~ Never mind. Anybody got any beer? He cracked his door open.

~ No way man, said the other boy. We don't even have a soda pop.

Del whistled and said, ~ This what I think it is?

The officer nodded. ~ Seventy-eight. Just got here

from Dee-troit. He revved the motor. Four-forty. Needs a little breaking in. Take care sister, he nodded to Milly. You too bro.

Turning his Fury onto Buckeye he accelerated with a short in-control squeal that got whistles of admiration from the young drivers.

~ Try it now? Milly got in and Del primed the carburator and the engine churned and sputtered and with an orange blaze under the hood it finally hit. Jesse slapped the cover back on and spun the wing nut.

~ You can let im out now Cans, said Del. Elvis, a little drunk on Candi's young perfume, wobbled out.

~ Get in here man. They squeezed Elvis into the dusty back seat of the Baker. Beads rattled under the rear-view mirror and they moved on out of the lights.

~ You got any food man? I'm jus dyin.

Jesse and Milly looked back over their arms. ~ How do you like your burgers?

~ I like em big.

Another patrol car swooshed by as they sat up on Camelback blinking to turn left into the Burger Joint. They went in and the fridges hummed and Jesse hit the kitchen light and the police band. ...Sskut skut. One-nine. Come in.

Sskut. One-niner I hear ya.

Sskut. You done checking down at the ranch?

Sskut, Raja. Lola says hyelloo.

Sskut. We got a rumor about the teddy bear over in

Los Gaddoze. You wan check it out?

Sskut. On my way, one-niner out. You could hear his tires going into a U-turn before he released the button.

~ Got a phone?

Jesse nodded. ~ Local?

~ Sure, said Elvis. I got lotsa friends around here. He dialed a one and mostly big numbers. The other end picked right up. Sam. You stayin up? Bet they're all freaked out, huh? Tell em I'm dead. Tell em I got a new girlfriend. Okay, stick with that then. No, fuckit I'm so fucked over I can't walk straight. I don' know man. Maybe I'll get some sleep. Hell if I know, jus a sec… Where are we?

Jesse frowned over the sizzling onions. ~ Who's askin?

Elvis looked hurt. ~ It's like you say, friends.

Jesse waved this off with his spatula.

Back on the phone Elvis said, ~ Ne' mind. Call you back later. Yeah, I'm in good hands. No, jus food. No. Yeah. No, no turning back. Yeah, I'm done. Well tell him to go fuck himself. Lemme re-phrase that. Tell im to go… yeah. Later.

Jesse warmed a plate on the grill and piled up fries next to a half-pound chili-burger.

~ How about a malt.

~ Peanut butter and bananas?

~ We got that.

~ Spooned, not sipped.

~ Comin up.

Jesse thought he heard piano notes under the hum of the mixer, and when he turned it off he heard Elvis singing. ~ Aye believe above a storm a smallist prair an shill-be heard... Evary tam ah heerr a nyewborn bebbi cra, or tudge a leav or see the skaa...

They pulled a table up next to the piano bench and Elvis went to town on the food. Jesse set his wide butt down next to Elvis's even wider one and ran through some chords. ~ Here's what you did on the record.

> Weh senz ma, bebby lef me, *Dint dint!*
> welah fondanew plaista dwell... *Dint dint!*
> weliz downathe iyenduv lonely streedatt
> Hardbreak hotelwheahwihbe dnt
> yamakemeso lonelybebby...

And then the bass went like this. *pohn pohn pa-pa-pahn...* And here's what you did in the show. *pown powng-powng pa-pa-pa-powng...* And was that you in the record doing this ivory thang? *padabbly dabbly doon* Cuz tonight you did this. *padidididid dee-d-d-debbly...* Mill, you feel like making up another burger?

~ Alright baby.

~ Extra pickles?

~ Extra pickles, Meem.

~ Alright. But sang it for him.

~ Naw. Jesse kept playing while he talked. You don't just sing for the king.

~ Why not? You jest as good as him. Better.

~ Naw, said Jesse. He kept playing while Elvis wolfed

down his fries. *Poong tink-tink-tink tink-tink-tink* Jever try this number?

Thehr is a rose in Spanish Haallum.

A red rose up in Spanish....

Stole this from King Curtis. *tink-tink-tink, tink.* And then there's always *binga-dinga-ding,* ba-le-lah, la-le-lah, la-la-lah-lah?

Theres-a-rose es black an Spanish Haahr-lem.

Aretha. ... It is a special one... But you could lower it down to here... *a-ronn ar-ronn ar-ron* And do it like this... There is a rrose...

Elvis pulled on his malt. ~Yeah. Yeah. You know, Benny called me when his single came out. No bull. King, this is Ben E King. Did you hear my record? I said, Yeah Benny, you sound great. You soun like me. And he laughed, Yeah I can't hit the high notes either. An he said, Listen I wanted to thank you for the song. I said, For what? An he says, What do you mean for what? Cause Jerry offered it to you first.

Elvis coughed. ~Fuck. I didn't even know about it. By the way, he says, who are you hangin out with? They don't even know who I am. I thanked him for the call. No man, thank you, he says. He musta thought I was some-kind-of idiot.

~Your... whadya-call-him? said Milly. Your curnel. He's the idiot.

~You got that f... You got that right mam. I could've had good new songs, stead of these damn left-overs. I could've made a classic movie. You know Jerry and Mike, they were putting together a movie for me. New songs, and maybe one a them Motown gals. But the colonel has a fit, your fans don' wanna see you messin with no black hussies. No offense mam.

~ I know where you're comin from.

Elvis slurped the bottom of his malt. ~ Can you see me and whas her name, Ronnie? Or Diana? We could've gone places. But thas all over now. Evrythings all over. Baby blue.

Milly frowned. ~ So who was that you jus called? Was that the curnel?

~ No, fuck no! Sorry. I shouldn't talk that way in front of you.

She patted his hand. ~ Thas all right Elvis. You got a right to be mad.

~ That was doctor Sam. My secret agent man.

Jesse hit an E-chord.

~ Secrut hunh, ayshun man. Secrut mm, ayshun man. They're givin you a numbah, an takin way yo name.

Elvis picked up a towel from the table and put it around his neck, groaned and turned himself back toward the keys. *tum, rummp. tum, rummp.* ~ You know this one?

Oh-well-om tahrd an so weary,

bud ah mus go alohng...

My mama loves that song, said Milly, bringing another heaped-up tray.

Jesse played the bass line while Elvis filled in the melody. ~ Your mama is still around? Where does she live?

Milly and Jesse looked at each other. ~ Tupelo.

~ Tupelo? No. What church she go to?

~ Babtist. Where else?

Elvis couldn't believe it. ~ That little church where sister Rose sings?

~ Rose been gone a long long time. An they moved the church up to Lee Street. When's the las time you was there?

~ I took Ginger down there a couple of... but you don' know her. Unhhh. He got up and walked across the room singing,

     ...Ord jus hopehnnn mine ahiies,

     nthet ahhy may seeee...

He dialed the phone. ... Yeah Sam. About a pig. Tupelo. Okay. Ready? Tupelo. The Babdis church on Lee Street. Yeah. Hold on. Mam? What's your mama's name?

~ Edna.

~ Edna. Yeah. Put, Lord if you lead me I cannot stray, love Elvis. Capidal Y. You, yeah. ... Rag, yeah, the works. Gotta go now, we're singin. ... Same to you.

Jesse moved over and Elvis sat down and took the bass.

     ~ ...Wontchoo lee-ee-ead mihhh.

~ Here's another one you played tonight...

~Tonight? Man, that seems like ages ago. Lez try this.

> …Eevning shadows mayik me blyue
> ha when each wairih day is thruu…

Milly put her hand on his shoulder and sang it low and slow like a lullaby.

> ~…Maa happiniss…

Elvis hung his heavy arm around her waist.

> ~…A millyun years it seems,
> have gone baa sense we shaaed our dreams…

She unwrapped his arm and laid him forward on the keys. ~He sleepin, poor baby.

MILLY SAT SIPPING COFFEE, reading the day-before-yesterday's Sunday paper. Behind her was Nizhoni's light presence, standing, unbraiding her hair. Near their feet a bulky man lay on a mattress under a Navajo blanket.

Beads clanked into a coffee can. ~ Donkey falls off rim, Milly read, lives to bray about it. Tusayan A Z, August nine, nineteen and sevenly-seven. Accidints can happen, even to the most sure-footed of creatures. Daniel Burnett was leading his two donkeys, Albert and Bob, onto the path down the south canyon wall when he felt a strange sensation. I looked behind me, mister Burnett said, and Bob was gone. Apparintly the donkey had tried to pass his brother, and either slipped or was bumped off the edge. Burnett hurried down the path, fearing he would find his donkey at the bottom of the canyon. When he turned at the second switch back, he heard the animal braying, and Albert brayed in return. Burnett hurried down, and found Bob standing on the trail, his side badly scraped but otherwise none the worse...

The phone rang. ~ Hello? This is Nizhoni. How are you, missis Martin? Really? No, it's not hot here yet. Going to be, uh-huh. Yes, I'm fixing her hair. Uh-huh. When you come out I'll fix your hair too. Uh-huh, here she is.

Milly took the phone. ~ Mornin mama. What? A bran new what? Slow down. Coop dee Vill? You mean a Cadillac? A converdible?

Milly stared at the man under the blanket. ~ No mama, no way. You keep it. Well read it to me…. Ahuh… Huh. See, it say to Edna. It don't say to no passer. It don't say to no Babtis church. You keep it. … Any where you want. Well if you don' deserve it who do? Yes I know mama, you did mama. No, I never said nothing. No honest, he don' know nothin about it. Jesse? No, he don' know neither. Elvis? Met him at a concert. Started talkin, asked me if I had a mama. No, he dint give me nothin. Hah, what I do with a big ol Coop dee Vill? Graceland? Thas up in Mempfis. Okay drive on up there. Maybe he be at home. No, take your girlfrens. Naw, ole weasel wount be no fun. Probly get jealous too. Take your girlfrens. No, Cadillacs got automatic. Probly jus a button. Yeah. Drive it aroun Tupelo first, then go up tomorra. Let her drive then, you practice first. Shoot mama, top down, live a little. Course you deserve it. Okay call me when you get there. Bye. Call me collect, save your money for gas. Love ya mama. Bye. Uh-huh. Bye.

Sunlight streaked across the pinewood floor, and a little boy came running in with a jar of beads in his hands. ~ Choya Choya. What did you bring me? Milly swept him up in her arms.

Nizhoni said, ~ Ready Milly? I have to wash your hair.

Milly followed her into the kitchen, scratching her head, her wiry hair going all directions. Choya came too. Water drummed and steamed in the sink. ~ Ooo oww! Easy, you gon burn me to death.

A woman came in the door, dressed traditional. She put her basket on a table, went to the unconscious man and looked him over. She took a red embroidered cloth from her rich black hair and laid it over his eyes. She said to him, ~ You have nice hair, but you're losing it. She searched in her apron and brought out a beaded pouch, opened it and took a pinch of stringy tobacco and sprinkled it on the blanket over the poor man's chest. Choya came out and stood next to her eating an ice cream cone, dripping on the man's shoulder.

Nizhoni led Milly as if she were blind from the kitchen back to her chair. She covered Milly's head with a big towel. ~ Ow, easy girl. Nizhoni dried her hair, smiling broadly while Milly moaned.

The woman brought out a stone jar and held it for Milly to smell. Milly breathed the subtle desert fragrance in and cooed with the pleasure of it, enjoying the woman's deep red-brown face. Nizhoni dipped her fingers in the jar and wet the shining spirals of Milly's hair.

Jesse came in and crossed the room with just the slightest limp. The woman pulled a chair from the table. ~ Azho inda.

She said it quietly but the sound of it startled Jesse.

~Auntie wants you to sit down, said Nizhoni.

Jesse sat down. ~ How come?

~ She wants to give you a haircut.

~What kind of haircut?

~An Elvis haircut, said the woman. She took Jesse's pony tail in her hand. Hold this.

Jesse looked at the three women looking at him. Nizhoni with her big early bloom of womanhood. Milly with half her hair twisted and waxed. Nizhoni's auntie with the desert smile and sharp scissors.

~Are you ready?

~ Two ham, one chili the works, one dry no lilies, said Carly, standing at the window in apron and cut-offs. One frazz big. Make that two frazz big.

~ Got it. That Billy?

~ Uh-huh, and Cindy.

~Whoa, somethin new. Who's next?

~ Delbert.

~And Candace?

~Yep. And Victry.

~ Tell em come in, would ya?

~ If you say so. Black and white pullin in.

~ Oh shit. Jimmy?

~ Can't tell. Sun's in my eyes. Might be Myron and

Sally.

Jesse put two more burgers on the grill and lifted the fry basket. Milly started the mixer. ~ I'll take those. Carly. Hurry up and bring the boys in. Don't worry honey, you're lookin fine.

~ Right here baby. Ham reg cheese. Ham chili. Frazz big. It's Myron all right. You start em baby I'll watch em.

Jesse called out, ~ Carly, got that sign made? Okay, chop-chop. Milly…

The side door squeaked. Victory came to the counter looking for Carly. Del and Candi went to gawk at the man on the mattress. His blanket was covered with loose tobacco, some half-empty packs, and even a half-carton of Luckies, and also a couple of bead bracelets and a black feather.

~ Hambo, whas happenin?

~ Del man, said Jesse, we got to move the body.

The boy's eyebrows jumped.

Jesse said, ~ He ain't dead or nothing. Jus sleepin it off.

~ Whoa, said Candi. How long's he been here?

~ Since Sunday morning. Listen, Myron only comes here when he has to take a piss.

~ Where we gonna move im to?

~ The john I guess.

~ Why dint ya move him to your house?

~ How was I sposed to know he was gonna sleep forever.

~Whoa, said Del. Candi, get the blanket. Wrap all this stuff up in it. Jesus, it's like one a them shrines down in Mexico. Vic, pull yourself away.

Candi picked up the blanket by the corners, uncovering the sleeping man, his bathrobe bunched around his waist, one slipper on, one off a bloated discolored foot. ~ Feeew.

~ Sure the old fucker ain't dead?

~ Here's the sign. Victory dropped it on top of Elvis, red magic marker on a box lid, OUT'VE ORdER. They grabbed onto the mattress and dragged it along and lost their grips and grabbed again.

~ Keep going, said Del. Put him in the girls.

~ How come? said Jesse.

~ Jesus yer dumb, said Del. Think about it.

A crooked smile appeared on Elvis's whiskery face.

~ The old fucker's enjoying the ride.

~ They're comin in, said Milly from the counter.

They curled the mattress and pulled and shoved it through the door. ~ Gahhh! The youngsters laughed when Jesse hit his back on the sink. ~ Goddam door won't shut. Victory kicked the foot of the mattress and they put the blanket back over Elvis and they all tried to go out at once.

~ Where's the frickin sign?

~ No time for that.

Delbert and Victory got to their table just as officer Myron came ambling in the side door, with officer Sally behind him. Myron headed straight for the john. Carly said, ~ The restroom's out of order, sir.

~ No prob, said Myron, holding up one finger. I'll use the sink.

Carly thought fast. ~ I think it's locked.

The rumble of a rusty toilet. Officer Sally, her hat under her arm, shaking her loose afro, was almost to the ladies door when the gents door opened and Candace came out, buckling her belt around the tight waist of her jeans. ~ Oh. You can use this one Sal… officer Brown. The womens is plugged up.

Out of the ladies came Jesse, red-faced. He taped the sign to the ladies door. ~ Dam kotex. Gonna hafta call the plumber.

~ I hear ya, said Officer Myron, and shifted to his other foot.

Jesse opened the mens door. ~ Who's first? Myron went.

Skuffing through the thin track of tobacco Jesse picked up a slipper and a pouch of Red Man on the way to the kitchen.

~ Where are we Mill?

~ We all right baby. Carly took the drinks out.

~ How're we going to keep this quiet?

~ Got to be free food. I got eight burgers on.

Officer Myron dropped his quarter in the jukebox and came back to the table singing along, ~ Now people doncha unnnerstan, the child needs a heppin hand… Sally had to concede a shrug of approval.

When Jesse came hatless out with the water Carly whistled and turned him around. ~Wow Jesse man. What happened to your hair?

~Not so old no more, said Victory.

~Elvis was here you know, Myron was saying. The chief saw him at the hosbidal. His old man was there too. Vernon Presley.

~I heard he went walking, said Sally.

~Naw. Some drug pusher started that rumor. Just to get us all runnin around so they could do their deals.

~Well, the chief bought it.

~What does that tell ya? Officer Myron laughed and tucked into his chili burger.

In the orange sunrise Milly came out of the old trailer house, a shopping bag under each arm. No traffic, only magpies checking the pavement for road kill. Time to breathe the cool desert air.

Inside the phone was ringing. She dropped her bags and hurried. Leaning over the air mattress where Jesse was sleeping, she pulled the phone toward her on the counter. ~Good… she coughed. Good morning.

A man's voice said, ~That's news to me. Sam here.

Milly sat down next to Jesse, who bounced a little and snored. ~Sam. Secret agent man.

A short laugh. ~ I see you've been filled in. This would be miss…

~ Miss Martin. Well Sam, how can I help you?

~ Miss Martin, oh yes. You would be Edna Martin's…

~ Daughter.

~ I see. Do you still have your house guest?

~ Yes I do. In fact I think I hear him. He may be up already.

~ Perfect. Listen, I have a call here from California. Tell him it's the dragon lady.

~ Okay, jus a minute… Milly heard the voice coming from the ladies room, where the door was propped open. ~ Elv…

He was sitting on the head, his face tilted down and his eyes nearly shut. He was singing.

> ~ Bm-bm-bm bm-bm-bm wise, men, know,
> when it's time, to, go… buh-buh-buh-buh-buh
> bud aa, cand, help, taking a dump, on, you.
> …like a sewer flows, shshurely to the sea,
> darrling so it goes….

The toilet bowl rumbled.

> …Some thangs, were, mint to be…

Milly hit the light, which switched on the fan. She held onto the feminine hygiene dispenser and held her breath.

~ So take, my, gland,

take my manager too, please,

cause aa...

Jesse groaned and turned over on his air mattress. He thought he heard a woman's voice on the receiver, which dangled near his ear. ~ Hullo?

~ Jesus El, why do you always do this? Are you alone?

~ Yea...

~ Try to give us a couple of seconds out of your busy life. All right?

Jesse sat up and scratched his head. ~ Yuh...

~ Jesus. Are you on something? Listen, Lisa is going to a movie with her friend. Born to Run, it's about a horse. She put on lipstick.

A pause. Jesse's sleepy hand searched for his missing pony tail.

~ Christ. Are you even listening? This is impornant. She says, Daddy lets me wear lipstick. So I'm putting her on, okay? Remember what we talked about?

~ Well, just a minute...

More opera from the toilet stall.

~ Shshlenk vee pffinkster-hunden.

Hart vee krapp shshtall!

Shshtinky vee brunnenshnitzel!

Milly already looked ill coming from the bathroom. Then she saw Jesse just sitting there looking at the receiver.

~ Oh, Jezuz Jess. Who is it?

~ First it was a woman. Now it's a little girl.

~ Ohhh… Milly's fingers spread over her heart. Well, talk to her.

~ Hello baby?

~ Daddy it's not even grown-up lipstick. It's that kind that glows in the dark.

Bending down with her ear next to the phone Milly whispered, ~ Say something.

~ …And Tiffany's mom lets her…

~ What color is it?

~ I have two kinds. One is pink. Real light pink. And the other is kind of orangy-pink. That's the one I have on, cuz it goes good with my jean jacket. And I have my glass-bead necklace on that you gave me. And Tiffany has white lipstick. Is it okay daddy?

Jesse looked at Milly, who made a face, palms up.

~ Sure baby, why not.

~ Really? Thank you daddy, I love you.

~ I love… Daddy loves you too baby.

A pause. ~ …Daddy? Mommy wants to talk to you. Love you.

~ Mussy den, mussy den,

zoom sheizzenkoff hinaus,

sheizzenkoff hind aus,

und du mein sheiss bleibst hier.

na na na na na…

~ Jesus, El, nice going. We talked about that specificly. Did you forget? That's the last time I'm goin to…

Are you there? Listen. The colonel called. All bent out of shape. Where's Elvis, he says. Like I'm supposed to be your help-maid or somethin. Listen, are you going to dump the sum-bee or not?

Milly nodded vigorously. ~Yeah, said Jesse.

~Good. We'll talk about it. They're all having a cow over at Graceland, all your so-called friends. I told them I'm not your messenger service. I don't see why you don't just kick them all out. Just tell your father... Listen, gotta go. Do you still love me?

Jesse looked at Milly in panic.

~...El?

Milly took the phone. ~...Hello, Miz Prizilla?

~...Yes?

~This is Elviz's nurse.

~...That had better be all you are, honey. Are you...?

~...Am I what?

Jesse stopped to stare at her, one leg in his jeans.

~Am I colored? Am I big and beautiful?

~Never mind honey, I can see you're not his type. What do you have him on? He doesn't sound good.

~Wann ik uhhh! wann ik uhhhh!

wann ik wieder wieder ahhh,

wieder wieder ngahhh!

und du mein sheiss plopst hier.

Nana-nananana...

Milly cradled her hand around the phone. ~He needs

a lotta tee-ell-cee right now. Well listen miz Prizilla I gotta....

~ Well listen have him call me. But not when... you know, not when he's high.

~ Aw right miz...

~ He's such a helpless little boy.

~ ...There's no shtring, upon this fart, of, mine, it was always sha na na na.

~ And he has no idea what school clothes cost nowdays.

~ ...Cause I don't have ay woood-en farrt.

Carly came in the side door, a big pink teddy bear under her arm.

~ No, well listen I gotta...

~ Yes I gotta run. Just remind him I'll be flying Lisa Marie out to Graceland next weekend. He's supposed to keep her for two weeks. His grandma will take care of her but just remind him, okay. He probably doesn't even know what day it is. Bye now.

~ Bye miz.... Whew, you got that right.

They found him passed out again. Waving the stink away Jesse flushed the toilet. Milly spread the blanket over him and tucked it under his bristly jowls, took the teddy bear from Carly and tucked it in with him. Feathered dream catchers turned in the breeze coming through the high window screen. Strings of beads hung over the mirror. Magazine pictures fluttered, taped to the wall, of Elvis in his army uniform, above a cluster of virgin Mary jars, candles flaming and guttering.

...Currently seventy-seven degrees on an August night in beautiful Arizona. Jesse mopped the floor, as he did six nights of every week of his life.

~ Night Carly. Night Victory. Milly's voice drifted in the door. The radio thumped on another station with the subdued sound of Victory's dad's Mercury, and faded into the night.

Swishing his mop back and forth on the bright floor, Jesse backed to the door. ~ Watcha doin babe?

~ Don't feel like coming in.

He leaned his mop handle against the wall, took off his paper hat and ran his hand through his hair. He found her looking out toward the mountains. ~ Thinking about home?

~ Not really. Back there the crickets are right nex to your feet. Here they come from all over, like a big warm universe is wrapped around you.

He slipped his arms around her. She rested her arms on his. Little cool stirrings in the air brought the smell of pollen from out on the desert floor.

...Time for something slow, said the deejay. This goes out to Kaja from Esther, away out there in White River. Wow there must be some stars out there tonight.

Dwandada dadada...

...Waaaiz, men, say, onlih fools rush in...

Somewhere a toilet flushed.

...bud aay cand help...

Milly turned around on tiptoe and embraced her man, fingers in his hair. ~ I like your new haircut. He held her closer and they stepped and swayed in the starlight.

...Shall ahhhi stay, wouldit beee a sin...

~ I don't limp when I'm dancin.

~ Hmm?

~ Baby?

~ Yeah Meem?

~ Scratch ma back.

~ Hmm? Like this?

~ Na, that tickles. Scratchery-er.

~ That better?

~ Difinitely.

She buttoned down her blouse and he reached in and scratched her back as they swayed under the stars.

...Take mai whohll life too...

~ A little higher.

~ There?

~ Up a little more.

~ I'll undo it.

~ Okay babe. Ahhh. Thas more like it.

...Like a hriver flows, shurrly to the seeea...

They turned around on tiptoe.

...Some thingz are, meantto be...

Close dancing under a river of starlight, they turned slowly and crossed a shaft of pale electric light. Over her partner's shoulder Milly saw the lonely silhouette in the doorway. He was shivering. She slipped from Jesse's arms and came toward Elvis, her breasts light brown above her loose black bra, arms reaching.

Milly sat on a couch in front of the TV, pick in her hair, sipping black coffee, papers spread out on the coffee table. ~ Groun beef's up again.

Jesse, in worn-out overalls, paused by the trailer house door. ~ Everything's up Meem.

~ And the girls are getting a raise. And the lectric bill…

~ What're taters doing?

~ Aint goin down Jesse. We gonna raise our prices?

~ One a these days.

~ How bout nex month when school starts? Dollar ninety for the basket?

~ Shees. If we gotta we gotta. The screen door swatted shut behind him.

…Stop it Ellie, stop it!

Oh, why did you have to stop me?…

In the TV matinee Elvis carried the bratty suicidal girl out of the blue water.

...Nobody cares about me, whether I live or die. Nobody seems to care, because you don't seem to care about yourself...

Milly tipped her glasses higher on her nose. Outside a car engine cranked and sputtered to life. Milly went over the bills, one eye on the TV. There was a knock at the other door, but she didn't hear. She wrote a check, ran the back of her wrist over her forehead and picked up another bill.

Another knock. ~ Anybody home?

She looked up to see a wiry little man standing on the rug. ~ Who the...?

~ Doctor Mann. We talked on the phone.

Milly pointed her pen at him. ~ Doctor or not, you...

~ Sorry miss Martin. The boss is still here, right?

~ Who...? Oh. He's in there sleeping. Like usual.

~ Yeah well look, I got some shi... stuff for him.

The doctor, if that's what he was, stood there with a black bag, eyes moving around like he was looking for a place to put it down.

~ Sit down.

This sounded like an order, and he took two steps to the blanket-covered chair and sat down on its front edge.

Milly walked through the little kitchen and rapped on the veneer. ~ Elvis. She cracked the flimsy door open. Elvis, somebody here to see you.

~ What? Who.

~ Says he's a doctor.

~ Tell im to go to hell.

~ What you say? You think thiz Milly's problem?

~ Okay, jus tell him to...

~ You... get yo fat ass outa bed.

~ Okay mama, don't...

~ An you better do it quick befo I throw it out on the road where it belong.

~ Okay mama. You in a bad mood or sumpin?

~ You aint seen no bad mood yet. Milly stopped in the kitchen. He'll be out in a...

~ Can you believe that? I mean why would they have him marry a chick like that? I mean look at her. Who can even believe that.

Milly glanced at the TV while she poured coffee. ~ Sometime they marry him up with some stiff ole white bee.

~ Yeah, that makes some sense. Cause he's like, you know the real Elvis, he's a lost little boy. He needs somebody ta reel him in.

~ Like that gal in Viva Vegas. That Tuesdy...

~ No that's Ann Margret. Now that I can understand. Sumpin you can hold onto. Now my gal, she's not very big, but she... oh thanks miss. Xactly what I need. Got any sugar? You know you remind me of a guy in our unit. He's a black guy. Was. Meek and mild as anything around the barracks, but get him out in the jungle? Like a goddam leopard. I made him my sargint. Frag insurance, know what I mean.

~ What kinda doctor are you?

~ Medical corps. You know, where they take away your rifle and put a big red target on your helmet? My gal was a nurse. Still is. She was born in the jungle. Right on the Meekong with cobras and evrything. Grew up barefoot. We were lost one time. Bird dropped us off and never came back. And we wandered in circles till the crotches rotted out of our...

Seeing Jesse at the screen door wiping his hands on an oil rag, the guest took a long drink of coffee and asked,

~ What kinda car you got? Sounds pitaful.

~ Fifty-four Baker.

~ Worst engine ever made. Carburation?

~ Yeah. Where were you, Viet Nam?

~ Yeah. You too?

~ Korea.

~ Like Nam with snow.

~ Sumpin like that.

~ You see any action?

~ Some.

The visitor drank the end of his coffee. Nobody rescued him from the silence, except the TV.

~ That gal is sposed to be native. Can you believe that? No hips, no cheekbones, just a little makeup and voila.

~ You that Sam guy? Secret agent man?

~ The same. You mister Martin?

~ Fuckin Sam! Elvis was up. What in the fuck you

doin here?

~ Brought you some shit Boss. Sam gave the black bag a shake.

~ Shit. Elvis hardly took his eye off the bag as he reached into the icebox. Bet that ain't all you come for Sam.

~ Come on now boss. Look, you said there's gonna be no turnin back, right?

~ What about it? The movie was over and there was a guy in an Elvis wig in a used car lot. The real king of rock and roll was spooning ice cream into his mouth from a cardboard gallon tub.

~ Well I been puttin somethin together. Somethin to make us all happy. Me included. Y'know that check you wrote to the policemen's hardship fund? Well guess what the chief's little woman is drivin now. Would you believe a bran new Lincoln?

Elvis scraped the bottom of the tub. ~ And?

~ And? And he owes us.

~ Fuck Sam. Whadyou mean us?

~ Just hold on boss. They got a guy on death row, up in Riverbend. He's a week short, follow me?

~ Fuck Sam I wouldn't follow you to the outhouse. Elvis looked at Jesse but Jesse wasn't smiling.

~ Come on boss, stay with me. You're the one that started me on this. You wanna disappear, right? Okay. I got it worked out. We did this in Nam. You got a dead body and a dead soul. You just change places. You play dead, an you disappear. Musical chairs. You blow taps and give the army the dog tags and who knows the diffrence.

Elvis licked the melted ice cream from the backs of his fingers.

Jesse said, ~ This ain't Nam, Sam.

~ You sure? You ever been there? I mean do you have any idea what goes on in the back of them private strip clubs in a punk town like...

~ What would he have to do? said Milly. Elvis here. What would he have to do?

Sam stopped and looked at her. ~ Okay. I'll be straight with you miss Martin. This is the only hard part. Cause when they hear that the king is dead Graceland is gonna be a war zone. Things will get out of control. So... we're gonna haf to drug him. Be just for a few minutes till we get him downtown. The rest is all covered. The chief...

~ What kinda drug?

~ It just knocks him out for a while. Slows the ticker. Makes the breathing...

~ His heart won't take it, Sam. There aint no way.

~ Look, it's only... I got some of it here in the bag. You can try it first.

Milly pulled Elvis over in front of the TV and he crumpled onto the sofa. ~ You're sposed to be a doctor. Look at him.

Sam stopped his mouth and looked at the ruin in front of him. ~ Yeah. Yeah, he's perty fucked up.

~ No thanks to you, huh?

~ Never mind, said Jesse. Sam, you must be hungry.

Come on, I'll fix you something to eat.

Sam sighed but popped right up. Jesse held the screen door open. Sam looked at his profile, and at Elvis on the couch with Milly kneeling next to him, and again at Jesse. ~Ahright. He bounded down the steps. Tell me mister Martin, y'ever been ta Memphis?

The TV was playing an Elvis special and there was the king in Vegas cupping the mike with all his rings, pouring out sweat, smirking, straining into the final note of a big song.

~ Get me the bag mama.

Milly pulled the doctor bag over and opened it. She took out a couple of plastic containers and squinted at them. She picked up her glasses from the coffee table. ~ Sec-onal. She read another one. Placid-il.

Elvis had perked up a little, his elbows on his knees, his eyes glazed over. ~ Get me some water to wash em down with. God ahm thirsty.

~ Baby, you can have some water, but you aint having none a this junk. Di-laudid? No wonder you so constipated. Baby you bin getting well. Don' go back now.

On TV the camera came down his jump-suited body and lingered below the waist, where a lump crept up from his crotch and reached for his big gaudy belt buckle.

The Elvis of now put his hands to his face and his big body shook.

~ Baby, you took your rings off.

~ I don' want em no more. I jus wanna die.

~ I know baby. I know.

And there was Elvis at the edge of the stage smirking, handing out bright silk scarves to middle-aged women reaching up in the sprinkle of his sweat, heaving out of their false-silk blouses, their husbands red-faced with the cocktails and the turn-on.

~ Go slow baby. I can't get a hold. She was straddling the big black seat behind him. With one hand she hugged the pocket of his leather jacket and with the other a huge windblown bouquet of white and red carnations. He answered by revving the motor and letting it pop. She leaned into his wide soft back as they climbed the hill. Once they had swung into Forest Hills they both sat up straight and he modulated the motor to a respectful chum.

~ Wow baby it is beautiful. The waking city of Memphis twinkled at a distant angle. The shocks shimmied as they rode through the colored section. They coasted onto the dewy lawn and under a line of trees.

~ Now aint this better? Aint you happy you brought the flowers yourself? Here. Tell miss Gladys it's the new you.

He took the long-stemmed bouquet and pulled himself up tall. Walking among the tombstones he passed a pile of fresh dark earth, and paused to look down into an open grave. Further on a slim marble Jesus, near life size, beckoned with open arms behind his mother. The headstone said

> ## GLADYS LOVE PRESLEY
> LOVING WIFE & MOTHER
> APRIL 25, 1912 – AUGUST 14, 1958
> SHE WAS THE SUNSHINE OF OUR HOME.

He set the flowers on the mound of the grave, went down on his knees, and took a couple of deep breaths, his hand holding his heart. ~ Mama you told me this day would come. I'm hauling this weight around, yeah, but just a minute ago I was a little boy and you had your arms aroun me. For a little while there everything went right. I never knew what I was doin though. And then you're gone mama and now I'm ready to go. You told me it would happen fast. Yeah mama I'm about ready. I'm gonna die. I couldn't tell you the God's truth if you were alive, it would break your heart. Did your heart use to hurt? My heart hurts mama like it was a rock in my chest. Could you kiss that away? I feel like you're with me. I feel washed in the spirit. Listen mama we got a plan. Now don't tell daddy just yet. We're gonna havta fool daddy one more time. But mama what you're gonna havta do is look down on Lisa Marie. Look down on my baby an guide her steps cause she's the one... Even though she's the strong one mama, I saw that as soon as she was born, but she's still gonna need you. Elvis sobbed. Happy birthday in heaven mama.

Milly heard a car door open. She heard talking and then whispering. Elvis felt a caress on his temples, lifting his face from the damp lawn, turning him over. Opening his eyes for an instant he saw the white thin arms of Jesus and the blue sky with little rosy clouds.

~ I can see it now. Death and life all mixed together. Uh-huh they stem from one another. I don't know where one…

~ Shhh. Hush now. Milly pulled his face into her bosom. He sighed and cuddled into her.

~ …Negra gal…

~ What they doin there?

~ …the Presley grave…

A siren made one spinning syllable. Frightened, she let his head down on her lap and straightened her sweater. Over by the mound of soil, by the new grave, a dozen or more people were standing. Lights were turning on a police car, and not far behind a long black Cadillac crept along.

A shadow fell over them and Milly looked up the brown-trousered legs of a big policewoman. ~ Is that you boss? Thought we might see you here today.

Elvis opened his eyes. ~ Oh, hullo off'cer Jodie.

A smile lit the face of Officer J. Clemente. ~ Did you have a nice visit? Come on then, I'll give yall a ride home to Graceland.

VERNON PRESLEY, MINT TEA CLINKING in his tall glass, was outside a little after one in the kind of heat that makes you want to hallucinate. A worker labored up the ladder and stepped onto the roof looking very unsteady. Vernon had to shake his head. ~ That fella's perty near as heavy as my son has gotten.

He went in the kitchen door of Graceland, into the air-conditioning that his son kept so cold it made everyone sick, and chatted with the maid as she fixed sandwiches for his mother and his granddaughter at the pool. He mentioned the Negro nurse that his son had hired when he was on tour out west. The maid teased him. ~ She aint yo type is she mista Prezley? Cause she sho aint Elvis kind a woman.

Upstairs in his son's bedroom Ginger sat in front of the dressing table in her white beach robe. She puckered her lips and applied some red lipstick. ~Well E. Aren't you going to say what you always say?

Glass-eyed teddy bears lounged in front of the mirror. The radio, tuned to the pop station WTNE, asked, ... Has anybody here, seen my old friend Abraham... Elvis lay on the bed in his wrinkled orange kimono, a paperback book balanced on his chest.

~ Say what mama?

~ Are you thinking about us?

~ Sure. But I'm reading right now.

~ Are you still reading that, what is that?

~ Shroud of Turin. Over there where Christ walked the earth. I'm gonna go there someday. They found the imprint of his body. Well, they think it is, anyway. Nail holes and everything.

~ You believe in that?

~ Boy's got to believe in something.

~ E? Her robe fell carelessly open as she turned toward him. You still want to marry me?

~ Course I do....

She sighed deeply and shook back her hair. ~ Then why don't you...

Ddrrringgg... Elvis picked up the phone. He glanced up at Ginger then looked down and answered, ~ Yuh?

El. Did you take the girls to the park?

~ Yuh.

Did Lisa have a good time? Is she up yet?

~ Uh...

El? Are you on something? Lisa says you've been acting strange, and...

~ Cill, I've been wanting to...

Listen El. A girl came into the shop today. I thought she might be shoplifting. One of these flower girls, she had flowers in her hair, the kind of white daisies I used to… I'm going to teach Lisa to make daisy chains if we ever… I'm not superstitious, you know that, but… Are you listening?

~Yuh. Yeah.

Well this girl says, the moon is in Pysees. Does that mean anything to you?

~ The moon? I saw it at the park. Lisa Marie said it had a face on it.

Ginger closed her robe and said, ~ Like a man singing. Like a man singing in the dark, was what she said.

Well, said Priscilla on the phone, guess what the girl said. Elvis? She said, missez Presley, some money will be coming to you. It will be like a miracle. She said like, but she meant it would be one. Can you believe it? I gave her some change from my purse. Not from the cash register. I know I shouldn't do that. But you know, it kind of shook me up. What do you suppose it means? Are you taking care of yourself? Maybe this tour will be better. But listen El, we can't meet you on the tour. Don't put ideas like that in Lisa's head. She's got to get ready for school.

~ Cilla.

What, Elvis?

~ I still…

You still love me? Listen El, you shouldn't say things like that if you don't mean them. Have Lisa call me, okay? Tell her mommy loves her.

Ginger, forgotten, folded her robe on the bed, and

caught a look at herself in the mirror. She turned side-ways and held her chin up a little higher. The hall door cracked open and Billy stuck his head in. ~ Hey-y. How's my cousin and his girl doin?

~ You barge in on me one more time William, and… She held the chair in front of her.

~ …An what, doll?

~ And somebody's going to have a dead cousin.

~ Ahright, knobby knees. Jus give this to yer lover-boy. It's from the doctor.

~ Don't get me mixed up in that… I've had it up to…

~ Hey, yer beautiful when yer… neckid.

Elvis put down the phone and made an effort to get up. ~ Billy, I'm gonna fucken…

~ Here cuz. Case ya need it. A small crisp paper bag flipped over and over in the air. Elvis raised his hand to catch it but it glanced off his shoulder and rattled with a plasticky sound on the floor under the window. ~ Hey, me an Jo got expenses ya know, an we…. Your old man says to wait till the end of the month. But we need clothes and shit for the tour, an…

~ I'll tell him. Now get the fuck outa here.

Billy stuck out his tongue at Ginger and hopped away laughing as the chair clattered into the doorway. She picked up her robe and looked up and there was Vernon standing in the hallway.

~ Scuse me, son.

Elvis stood up groaning. ~ Come in daddy. God I wish I wasn't so heavy. Just a sec. You decent, Ginge?

Ginger had thrown her bathrobe on and was tying it. Elvis said, ~ Come in daddy. I wanted to talk to you. How ya doin this morning?

Vernon set the chair upright. He looked his age with his strawberry-white hair, but in the cuffed linen trousers that broke over his saddle shoes he still walked like a young man. ~ Afternoon, son. Listen…

~ Just a minute daddy. Ginge, where ya going?

~ To run my bath.

Elvis reached for her wrist, looking around in a sudden panic. ~ Stay here while we talk.

~ Why? she said. Her eyes went to Vernon's blank face, back to Elvis's agitated face.

~ Maybe we'll talk about the wedding.

~ But I told you…

~ Jus do me a favor.

She crossed her arms and sat on the bed.

~ Colonel's been callin, said Vernon. Leven days till the tour he says. Wants to know if you're ready. We need the money he says. Can't afford no more fiascoes. That kinda stuff. He's been gambling if you ask me.

Ginger started to get up, but Elvis detained her.

~ Says we owe him two million and he wants a hunerd grand of it right now.

Elvis's eyelids fell and the side of his mouth turned up in a grin. ~ Man, I'll be glad when…

~And did you tell Billa he could have twenny thou?

~ Damn Billy. Give him thirty and tell him to get lost. Tell him forget about the tour.

Ginger rose from the bed, re-tying her robe. ~ I hope you mean it this time Elvis.

Vernon was still full of bad news. ~ Look, this heah roofin crew...

~Yeah, said Elvis, thinking. We won't hire them again. He put his hand on his father's shoulder and walked him toward the door. Daddy listen. I been thinkin bout you an mama an the good times.... an the hard times.

His voice was thin and he stood there slouching, a strange disappointed fat man in a bright robe, and put his arms around his father's neck. Patting him fondly his father said, ~ Thas all right son. Gonna be better times. You'll see. Vernon paused to look at his boy once more before he closed the door.

Elvis stood like he was in a daze. Then, as if he just remembered Ginger was there he said, ~ Ginge, why don't you take a bath and relax.

Ginger looked at him strangely. ~ So much for the wedding.

~Ah Ginge. Give your man a kiss.

She folded her arms. ~ I'm too damn mad right now. Elvis this has just got to...

Elvis reached for her elbow. ~ Don't be mad, mama.

~All right E. But don't you see why I can't marry you? She kissed him quickly on the lips and went into the hallway to her bathroom.

Elvis wandered over to the big window.

If you looked in through the windows of Graceland you would see the King in his shiny robe on a clammy hot August day and he would be looking out past you over Elvis Presley Boulevard. He would turn and pick up his paperback from the super-king-sized bed that he bought for his wife Priscilla. Ex-wife. He would look past that to the hallway door Ginger had left open on her way to the other bathroom. Her bathroom now. There are days when he urgently wants to marry her. He turns and goes into his own big bathroom. If you were shadowing him around, you would hear a little clatter from an old-fashioned key that dangles by a string from the brass door knob. He goes to the sink and faces the big mirrors of a double-wide medicine cabinet, pulls back his slumpy shoulders, pushes his hand through his hair and tries to find himself in the reflection. Doomed, is what he is thinking. Doomed. Behind him is the toilet, where he spends a lot of time these days, and a reading rack next to it. To his left is a big shower where stripey big-eyed fish swim on an island-blue shower curtain. The door beside the shower is shut. It goes to another bedroom, that used to be where the bodyguard slept. It's a nice room, not all cluttered like the rest of the house, with tall windows on two sides and twin beds. Just for now the room belongs to a miss Milly Martin. If you asked her about herself she would say she was kind of a homely black nurse from Mizzippi, well, not a nurse officially but playing the role capably. That's why she has come with Elvis to Graceland. Because Elvis hasn't been well for – well, they say his troubles started when his mother passed away, which was… seventy-seven take-away fifty-eight is…. The room has a nice old radio with lots of bass and Milly has it tuned to WDIA, Memphis soul, Lucille singing the Thrill is Gone. She is wearing a loose cotton blouse over polyester slacks and a pair of flip-flops, looking out the side window between the long gauze curtains. From here she can see the quivering willow tree and the swimming pool, Elvis's grandmother reading under an umbrella and his daughter playing in the turquoise water. A blurry wisp of the child's voice comes in with a breeze that lifts the curtains. A noise intrudes from behind the closed door, a little noise but strange, and Milly turns, her hand over the ruffle of her blouse.

In the bathroom with Elvis, above the shower curtain, a black rectangle appeared in the ceiling. A lithe dark figure lowered itself without a sound, dangled for a moment, and – ponkk – landed softly on the tiles, and slipped past the curtain and over the short tile wall. He wore a carpenter's hat and trim black overalls. ~Where is she?

Elvis was sitting on the toilet, absorbed in his paperback. ~That you Sam? Thanks for knockin.

Sam crept catlike to the door and peered through the keyhole. A dozen steps away Ginger, in a bath towel, was getting something from her dressing table.

~ What's she doin?

~ Takin a bath.

~ How long will she be in there?

~ Forever. Elvis laughed down in his throat. At least.

A tapping on the opposite door.

~ Jus a minute, Mill. The toilet paper bar rattled and Elvis wiped his ass. There was a cough from up above.

Sam let Milly in. ~ Looks like it's a go, miss Martin.

But Elvis was suddenly in a sweaty panic. ~ Hold it right there. We're not goin through with this.

Milly peered into his face and said, ~ Baby, you the one got to decide that.

~ Where's Lisa Marie?

~ She's out by the pool, with gramma Presley.

~ I can't let her... I gotta say good-bye to her.

~ Elvis, you can't...

Elvis stopped himself with an effort and sat his weight down on the wall of the shower.

~ Baby, are you okay?

~ Boss, said Sam. Boss, this is it. You want me to give you something?

~ God, Sam. Milly got between them.

~ She's gonna lose her daddy, said Elvis.

~ Baby, remember, we talked about it. You're too sick to be a good daddy.

~ Thas what Priscilla says.

~ Well, she's right this once. You're gonna get well.

When she's old enough we'll send for her.

~ What about gramma? I should've…

~ It's now or never boss, Sam cut in. The show's starting.

Elvis took a deep breath. His hand felt for his medallion and grasped it tightly. Milly stayed at his side, propping him up.

~ We gotta move, said Sam. Martin, come on down. Bring my bag with you.

A clanking of aluminum and the rungs of a ladder descended through the gap above the shower curtain. A pair of dirty socks appeared, then a hefty butt in new black overalls, then a broad back and a head of black hair that curved down to the nape and broke over the collar like Elvis's hair. These parts disappeared in turn behind the wiggling tropical fish. The curtain parted and there next to the ladder stood a ruined Elvis look-alike.

Elvis himself unhunched his shoulders like he was seeing himself in a mirror and didn't like what he saw. The face was fishy gray, enough to make you smell a morgue in a heat wave. The hair was his hair. The eyes were his astounded eyes.

~ Jess?

~ Damn, said Milly. You two do look alike.

~ It's the make-up, said Sam, fiddling with the contents of his black bag.

~ Say something baby.

~ Shit, Mimi. I don't feel so good.

~ It's the valium, said Sam. Martin, you get outa that outfit and sit down here. Boss, give im your kimono.

Both of them complied. Jesse pulled off his overalls and stood there in his boxers. Elvis, less agile, had trouble undoing the knot in the silk belt around what used to be his waist and Milly had to help him. Jesse tried on the nice silk robe and looked in the mirror. Elvis sat on the tile wall and stared at the overalls he was supposed to put on. Milly picked up one of his feet.

~ Ow.

~ Baby, you all bloated. Look like my mama's feet. She pulled the pant leg on as gently as she could.

Sam pulled Jesse to the toilet and powdered his gray face. ~ Just a little touch-up. Boss, give im your chain. Come on, come on. Rings too. Sam snapped his fingers.

Milly abandoned the overalls and began pulling at Elvis's rings.

~ Ow. Leave that one on, said Elvis. He can have the rest. Fuck em. Ow.

~ Let's see your veins now, Martin. Sam rolled up the sleeve of the kimono and examined Jesse's arm. Nice. He brought a syringe out of his bag.

~ Jezuz. Milly had opened the mirrors above the sink. You got a whole drugstore here. Where's your vazeline?

~ Uh... Elvis, overalls half-on, tried to think.

~ Oh wait... Milly went out, found her purse and emptied it onto her bed.

Sam held Jesse's elbow. ~ This ain't gonna hurtcha.

Just gonna knock you out and slow your heartbeat till we get you to the morgue. He was squinting at the syringe as Milly returned with a green jar.

~ You aint gonna bury me. Are you?

~ No baby, he aint gonna bury you. Are you Sam?

Sam laughed. ~ Nah, I got a stiff in last night from the state pen. Got im all made up, layin in the cooler, just waiting for the box. Just a little poke.

~ Sam, are you sure…?

~ Ow, jeesh! Jesse held his arm.

~ Look, said Sam, stowing the syringe back in his bag. We been all through this. Boss, you got the stuff?

Elvis stared at him blankly.

~ Damn! We even practiced this. Bread and shit. Bread and shit. You know the words to what, two thousand songs, and you can't remember bread and shit?

Elvis looked as drugged as Jesse. Both their mouths formed the words, Brd n sht, brd n sht.

~ Boss, wake up. Din't Billy give you some pills?

~ Oh, yeah. So shoot me. Ow!

Milly had screwed off another of his gaudy rings.

Sam peered through the keyhole. ~ Okay, okay. I'll go in and get em. Where the fuck are they?

~ Ow. Calm down Sam. Look under the mattress. And the pills… uh…

~ I'm goin in, said Sam, and slid through to Elvis's bedroom. He slunk to the super-king bed and lifted the mattress, reached under and came up with a flattened paper sack, peeked in and sighed like a man smoking a fresh Montecristo. Then he turned this way and that, tiptoeing around the bed, searching.

Jesse, sitting on the toilet seat, had begun to sag and tip. Milly noticed too late. He swayed and fell to the floor with a heavy plop.

Sam jumped like a snakebit rabbit.

~ Elvis? It was Ginger's voice.

Sam froze. He heard her bathroom door open. ~ Elvis? What happened?

Sam clasped the paper sack to his breast and dove under the bed.

Milly was on her knees over Jesse's body. ~ Jesse? Talk to me baby. Jeezuz Jesse, can you hear me?

Jesse's eyes opened and rolled. ~ Mimi? His arm reached, then flopped to the pine board floor. ~ Doh le ub bury me.

~ No baby, no. Milly was crying.

~ Elvis! The young woman stood in the bedroom, dripping, a towel in one hand.

Milly whispered urgently, ~ Talk to her!

Elvis stood up and swayed, overalls around his fat knees. Milly, anticipating, was on her feet. She grabbed him and shook him. ~ Talk to her.

Elvis laughed out loud.

~ Elvis goddammit. D'you mind telling me what happened?

~ I dropped my book, mama. Doin' some heavy readin.

~ Very funny Elvis. I'm standing here in the cold, and now the floor is all wet.

Milly shook him again to keep him from laughing. ~ Ah'm sorry mama.

Wagging her head, Ginger tucked the sheets in the foot of the bed and spread out the bedspread. ~ You think you're sorry.

Sam watched her bare feet walking away. Peeking out, he saw her pink globes and tan shoulder blades with the white strap lines. When he heard her bathroom door click shut, he backed into Elvis's bathroom.

~ Look Sam…

~ Listen boss, you're gonna hafta go in an find that shit.

~ Sam, look man, why don't we jus forget about it?

But Sam was in a panic. ~ You don't get it. We hafta give em a C.O.D.

~ A what?

~ A cause of death.

Elvis and Milly looked at the body on the floor.

~ Boss, we gotta get this off ya. Sam started to yank at the overalls that were up around Elvis's knees, but Milly pushed him away. She started to coax the cuffs off his ankles. But then Sam knelt on the floor and started pulling on Jesse, and she left Elvis and helped him roll Jesse's limp body.

~ Take the robe off him. Damn. Boss, you gotta find the shit, ahright? The coroner's report is already written up. Coronary fibrillation, complicated by an OD of methiqualone.

~ Compli-what?

~ Quay-lude.

~ Yeah. Elvis went into the bedroom, went to the window and gazed out, fiddling with his robe. Remembering, he looked around on the floor. He tried to get down on his hands and knees, but his body was too stiff and heavy.

~ I wish I really was dead. Mama?

Elvis went into the hallway, trying to hurry. He turned the knob on Ginger's bathroom door and cracked it open. Steam leaked through the crack. ~ Ginge?

Ginger sighed out loud. She was soaking in the tub. ~ Elvis, I told you... Oh well, as long as you're here, hand me my razor, will you?

Elvis looked around.

~ There on the sink, right in front of you.

She soaped her leg before taking the razor from him. ~ Looking for something else?

~ My pills?

Ginger ran the razor down her long smooth leg. ~ That junk Billy threw at you?

~ Yeah.

~ You told me you were done with all that. You swore it.

~ I am, but...

~ But just one last time, huh. She sighed again. This one's dull. Put a new blade in, will you?

Elvis stared at Ginger's shape as she handed him the razor. His hands shook trying to open the blades.

~ Here, I'll do it myself. It's there in the wastebasket. If you need it that much you can just scrounge for it like a bum.

Elvis went through the tissue and hair and kotex, found the little bag. It rattled when he shook it. ~ Thanks mama. How long you going to be in here?

~ Ow. Damn Elvis, can't you leave me alone?

~ Okay. Ahright. I'm gonna go do some reading.

~ You do that. Close the door behind you.

The Year of the Cat played on Ginger's radio. Back in Elvis's bathroom Milly knelt beside Jesse's body next to the toilet. How long has this been going on? drifted in from Milly's bedroom.

~ Got it, Boss? Whew. We gotta sit im up. Come on, help me.

Milly was weeping.

~ Hold his head up. Sam's hands fumbled with the container.

~ Sam, you're freakin out. Give me that.

Jesse's head fell forward. Milly poured the contents out in Sam's hand, a large yellow pill.

~ One freakin pill?

Elvis had to laugh. ~ Don't have a cow Sam. You knew fuckin Billy would swipe em.

Sam was too livid to even swear. ~ Here, put it in his mouth.

~ What?

~ Under his tongue, come on. Boss, gimme your kimono.

~ Huh?

Sam grabbed the overalls and tossed them at him. ~ Put these on.

~ I can't get em on. Don't you see, I'm too fuckin fat.

Milly lay Jesse back down, his head bumping on the floor, and hurried into her bedroom.

~ I'm a goddam blimp, Elvis was saying.

~ Okay okay. Don't have a heart attack.

Milly came back with a bed sheet and threw it around Elvis's shoulders. ~ Here baby. Give your robe to Sam.

Robe in hand, Sam said, ~ Ahright boss, you're all done. You can go up now. Miss Martin, put the kimono on your brother and we're outa here.

Elvis went into the shower. With difficulty he started up the ladder.

~ All right now, roll him over. Yeah, face down. That's it. Okay pull off his shorts.

~ No Sam.

~ Come on come on, we gotta stay with the plan. Now be ready to call emergency. Remember, it'll be taped.

Milly went to her bedroom, put her things back in her purse, and started remaking the bed. Sam reached in his overalls and took out a cigar.

Elvis, halfway up the ladder dressed only in a silk sheet, looked down on the scene. The body lay next to the toilet, silk kimono gathered on his back, a green dragon fake-tattooed across his round buttocks.

Elvis climbed another couple of steps, and then his foot slipped. He just about caught himself, but he lost control and swooned backwards like a milkshake tipping off a tray. The ladder shook and rattled, the tiles rang like a stone bell, and his big body crashed to the floor, taking Sam down with him.

Milly rushed in, threw herself down next to Elvis and cradled his head.

~ Elvis! Ginger, in shorts and bra, came running. Sam lunged for the key and turned it in the lock.

Ginger rattled the knob and shrieked, ~ Elvis?

Elvis moaned and sat up. ~ Fuck. Milly, get me the fuck outa here.

Sam sat paralyzed with his back against the door. ~ You can't let em catch us like this. They'll put my ass in a sling you wouldn't…

~ Shut up Sam.

Elvis picked himself up. He seemed lighter than before.

~ Elvis! Ginger was hysterical. Elvis, are you in there?

Sam got up holding his back. ~ I don't hear the police. Are they coming? Awwwhn, my fuckin…

~ I couldn't get through, said Milly. She… was on the phone, and then she dropped it on the floor.

But then a far-away siren sounded. Elvis started up the ladder again, the beautiful turquoise dragon waggling on his doughy ass as he mounted the rungs. Milly reached up. ~ Don't fall baby.

The ladder creaked and shook, and Elvis was gone. Sam lurched up the rungs after him, and in a moment the ladder was knocking against the shower bar and disappearing, and the hole in the ceiling went from black to white.

The sirens were coming closer. Pulling her eyes away from Jesse's unconscious body, Milly saw the clothing that was scattered around the floor. ~ Sam, wait! Sam must have had the same thought, because the hole opened again. She picked up the paper bag and wrapped the overalls around it. She heard footsteps on the stairs. She stretched on tiptoe and a frantic hand snatched the bundle. She picked up the sheet and held it to her breast. A couple of bills fluttered down as the ceiling closed up.

~ Son. Vernon Presley, with Ginger at his elbow, stood in the doorway turning pale as a ghost. Son.

Milly stood over the body. ~ Don't look. It's too horrible.

Ginger tried to come close, bent over and moaned pitifully.

~ Oh no, son! Vernon sobbed.

Ginger's little body convulsed. Amber liquid spewed

from her mouth and splashed off the edge of the toilet. Milly caught her, feeling strangely sorry for her. With the wadded sheet she wiped the vomit from the trim bronze legs and the painted toes in their expensive sandals. She was blocking Vernon's view and keeping him away from the strangely peaceful face on the floor. Vernon knelt next to the body and tugged the robe over the two big mounds of tattooed flesh.

A policeman burst in, a slim young straight-arrow. Then officer Jodie Clemente. ~ Everyone out, she ordered. Make room for the medics. Weed, get em out of here.

Billy had pushed his way into the doorway. ~ No! he said. This can't happen. He wouldn't of even felt it. There's no way!

Officer Jodie was dealing with Vernon. ~ Wait here in the bedroom, mister Presley. The medics are on their way.

Young officer Weed looked the body over. ~ It's him all right. He looks like shit.

~ God. Jodie folded her arms and shivered. Is it always this cold in here? She stooped down next to the body. She pulled the wrist out from under the belly. Subject's still warm though. Lookit all these rings. When did this happen? Weed? Do they know anything?

~ The girl… Young officer Weed's voice shook. The girl said she heard a noise.

~ How long ago?

~ She doesn't know. Pretty mixed up. Looks like the coroner is here.

~ Thank God, said officer Jodie. Doctor Casey? Oh...

The man coming into Elvis's bathroom was small and wiry, dressed in a dark suit, carrying an old-fashioned doctor's bag. ~ I'm Doctor Mann, he said. Doctor Casey is on vacation.

~ Doctor Mann, we got a bad situation here.

~ Officer Clemente, he said, looking at her nam tag. How long have you been here?

~ We just got here sir. We were in the neighborhood.

Doctor Mann went to the body and began examining. ~ Got a pulse?

~ No sir.

~ Did you check his airway?

~ No sir.

~ Do that please.

~ Yes sir. Jodie Clemente went down on one knee and turned the face to one side.

Doctor Mann took a stethoscope out of his bag. ~ Get those people out of the doorway, he said. But nobody moved, waiting for the verdict.

~ Ugh. Bad news here. Officer Jodie held up a large yellow capsule.

A moan went up at the doorway.

Doctor Mann moved his stethoscope from place to place on the back of the wrinkled robe. When he looked at his watch the weeping began. ~ Time, thirteen-forty-two. Probable cause of death... Officer Weed, close these doors.

~ No, Elvis no.

The young officer, his lip quivering, pushed back the stricken throng.

~ Help him, officer Clemente.

While they were so occupied, the doctor looked intently at the ceiling above the shower. The door closed and the sound of moaning stopped. ~ Got a report form?

~ Yes sir.

~ Get to work then. Any witnesses?

~ The girlfriend, said officer Weed. And the father, he just couldn't believe his son would... And that nigra nurse, where'd she go?

~ We'll get statements. Now case the scene. Keep your feet outa this vomitus.

~ We need more light. Weed tried one of the wall switches next to the reading rack. A popping sound, and the big screen lit up in the veneer console a couple of yards in front of the toilet. ... Memphis police asking the public to avoid going near Graceland mansion, in the south part of town off Highway 51. We return you now to your regular programming.

...But Nancy, don't you see, it's for her
own good.

...I'm just afraid... afraid you're going to push
her away... and we'll never see her again.

~ Look at that. The sumbitch watched TV sitting on the john.

…But don't you see darling? She'll thank
us later. He's just a young hoodlum from
Pinemartin…

Officer Jodie inspected the torn shower curtain. Something on the shower floor caught her attention.

~ There's the pill bottle, said officer Weed, behind
the john here. He took out his night stick and batted the
plastic thing toward his feet.

Jodie went into the shower, stooped and picked up
something that looked like a dollar bill, but when she
looked at it her mouth fell open.

~ Let me see that, said Doctor Mann.

Officer Jodie froze. But seeing the two men's backs
she picked up another bill and pulled in a deep breath
and stuffed them into her watch pocket. ~ Hey, here's a
bar of soap. Want a couple of Elvis's pubic hairs for your
collection?

~ God, said Weed. Let's just get this done before I
puke.

Jodie picked up her clipboard. ~ What do we have
so far?

~ A pill bottle, said Weed.

~ Good. What else?

~ We got barf all over the place. Maybe he choked
on it.

~ Good. What did he have for breakfast?

Weed coughed. ~ I gotta get some air.

…Sskut skut. The coroner hooked his stethoscope

around his neck and grabbed his radio. ~ Mann. Go ahead. … Roger that chief. I'll send a man down. Out. Sskut. Officer Weed, go down and get a body bag.

~ Yes sir, thank you. He started to go out past the shower.

~ That way. Down the stairs. They'll meet you there.

…Mmm … aah ah ah…

Milly's bedroom radio was pleading,

Don't, leave me this way-ay-ay-y-y

… aa cant suhvi-ive, cant stay yalive…

~ Okay Clemente let's get this buttoned up. The police are downstairs talking to mister Presley. Him and the girl gave them a positive ID. Did you describe the subject?

~ Were we sposed to?

~ Just write this down. Subject prone on floor next to commode. White male, early to mid forties, medium height, heavy set. Wearing gold kimono, rings, excetra. Got that?

The policewoman wrote as fast as she could. The mute TV had cut away from As the World Turns to show pictures of Elvis. A black-and-white of the kid in his army uniform. The singer with the hound dog. The king practicing karate.

~ …Face bloated. Pills found in mouth. Vital signs negative. No sign of foul play. Got it?

Officer Weed came back with the body bag. More orders from the doctor. ~ Weed, go down and guard the stairs. Don't let nobody come up. I mean nobody.

~ Right sir. He paused to look at the TV. God. A sky shot, Graceland mansion, picture shaking, surrounded by green, zooming in, cars at all angles on the drive, shaking some more.

> ...Unsubstantiated rumor that Presley,
> age forty-two...

Doctor Mann rolled the body. ~ Slide it under, Clemente. Ahright, now the other way. The body lay on the open bag, face up. Mann found a smashed cigar and slipped it into his pocket.

~ It's a sad day in Memphis. The voice belonged to a woman in the doorway, a slim woman in a green pants suit.

~ It's a sad day everywhere, said officer Jodie.

~ Who the hell are you? said Doctor Mann.

~ A reporter. From a national publication.

~ They'll be no photographs taken here.

~ I'm only sorry I didn't bring my camera man.

~ Officer Clemente, take the report downstairs.

~ Yes sir. She picked up her papers, turned around and checked the watch pocket of her too-tight police trow, and went out.

The reporter closed the door behind her.

Mann pulled out his radio. ~ Look, I can have you arrested.

~ Lieutenant Samuels, said the reporter. Or should I call you Doctor Mann? One way or the other, we're onto you.

~ I just… What do you want?

Milly came quietly in the other door.

~ Just a little information.

Milly knelt over the body. Lovingly she pulled the stiff plastic over the suffering face.

~ What kind of inform… We got a positive ID. The poor bastard OD'ed, all right? Methi…

~ Genetic information.

~ Listen, all I want to do… All I want… Look, I just want to go back to Cambodia. I just want to see my wife and…

~ We know all that, Samuels. We twisted the chief's…

~ What do you want with him? Milly broke in.

~ Just a little tissue.

~ What kind of tissue?

~ A little thing called DNA?

Sskut, skut. ~ Chief. We got a mayday. Chief?

The reporter stood her ground.

~ Sam, said Milly. Get a hold of yourself. She's got you dead to…

~ But I can't… Skut. Doctor Mann went down on his knees.

~ Let her have what she wants.

~ But she'll check the DNA and…

Milly pulled a limp arm from the body bag. ~ Here, take your tissue.

~ …And she'll find out that…

~ Criminy, Sam. Be cool.

The woman took something from her pocket and pressed it into the flesh of the middle finger. Click! The bare feet shuddered, the toes curled and then relaxed.

The reporter was looking at her sample. ~ Thank you.

~ ...She's going to prove that this guy isn't...

~ Sam. Can it.

The reporter stopped in the doorway, the evidence in her hand. She opened her mouth as if to gloat, but Milly stood up and faced her.

~ Thank you, said the reporter again, and was gone.

    ...Train ah rra-a-ide, sixtee-een coaches
    loh-o-ong...

Doctor Mann stood by the shower, his hands on the cool tiles, hyperventilating. The other door swung open and a big man in a white suit walked in. ~ How we doin Sammy? We gon make it?

~ I dunno, chief.

~ Whad'ya mean ya don't know? We got a problem?

~ Listen chief, I'll get im planted in the box, and then you'll never see me again.

~ That's fine Sammy. Ya done good. Jus one more lil detail. He rubbed his thumb and fingertips together.

Behind the chief of police's white-suited back, Milly sat on the floor and held Jesse's hand. ~ Gonna be dark for awhile baby, but don' worry. We gonna be in a nice motel tonight. We gonna watch TV till you feel better. She patted his hand and tucked it in.

A loud knock. ~ Medics!

The chief, one hand still in his pocket, opened the door for them. ~ Gentlemen. He nodded to the body bag. You're just a little late.

~ Fifty-one is a zoo, chief. We had the siren going, but...

~ Don' worry bout it. Poor sumbitch was already gone. Probly clocked out before he fell off the can.

Other officers crowded in the doorway, and a man in a lab suit with an old-fashioned flash camera. The paramedics set the pallet on the floor and regarded the bulging bag with the feet sticking out. ~ Drugs?

~ Fraid so.

~ He was always a friend to us.

~ Amen to that. Officer Weed, choked up with grief or nausea, pulled out his handkerchief.

A child squeezed through the thicket of legs, a little girl in a blue bathing suit, and stood there looking all alone, wet and shivering, next to the big lifeless bare feet. ~ Something's wrong, she said with eerie calmness.

~ Get her out of here, barked the doctor.

~ Get the little girl out of here, said the chief. Don't let her see her daddy like this. Weed, zip im up.

~ Something's wrong, the little girl repeated.

~ Come on sweetie. Officer Jodie scooped her up in her arms.

Over the policewoman's big shoulder the little girl kept

saying, ~ Something's wrong... not my daddy!

A needle squawked on the vinyl.

    ...We interrupt this... WDIA has received a report that Memphis recording star Elvis Presley has been found dead in his... The voice stuck in a sob. In his bathroom at Graceland.

The mike stayed open while a chair scuffed. There was dead air, and soon a pop and hiss and familiar notes, and Elvis sang,

    Oh well uhm tarrrd an so wea-r-ry,

    but ah mu-us go alo-o-ng...

In the other bedroom a shaky voice was saying, ... Incredible tragic news from Graceland. ...Waiting for a confirmation from the Memphis PD...

    ...There will be peace in the valley

    for me-ee-ee some day...

Elvis sat in the attic, all the voices coming up to him, his father sobbing out loud like at his mother's funeral, his daughter insisting, ~ I'm going to find my daddy! trying to get someone to believe her. He listened for his grandma's voice, but didn't hear her. He listened for his mother's voice. ~ Son, son.

    ~ ...An awful noise. That would be Ginger, answering questions. Scared me half to death.

    Clear voices right below him. ~ Toilet top been down this whole time?

    ~ Shit. Whatcha got there?

    ~ Paper, kinda scummy. Coupla turds. Like lil tootsy

rolls.

    ~ Plugged up, huh?

    ~ Like an apple in a tailpipe.

Muffled shouting outside. Sirens from every direction.

    ~ What about this dirty sock over here?

    ~ The fool had his robe on inside-out.

      ...I promised myself to treat myself

      and visit a nearby tower...

The chief was giving the lowdown, ~ ...Heart attack. Yes. No, just prescription drugs. Under a doctor's care, yeah. Yesterday was the anniversry of his mother's death. Lot of pressure getting up for another tour, that kind of thing. More than that, we can't speculate.

    Father father, everybody thinks we're wrong...

    ~ Hah hah. I told you don't slip in the barf. Hey here's sumpin rich. This fat-ass had grapefruit for breakfast. Pink grapefruit...

    ~ ...Tragic. ... A great friend of law enforcement... Donated thousands... Can't tell you how much we'll... How much the world...

    ~ We were planning to get married, Ginger was saying.

    Sskut. ... Prezley Boulevard's all jammed in. Affirmative. We brought the ambulance down the sidewalk. Skt. No shit Sherlock. Listen, they wanna go through the flowers but they need your okay. ... Okay we're gonna come on through. Twenny-two out.

…Full investigation…

…Priscilla Presley, widow of the deceased,
flying in from Calif…

~ I don't know Curnel, I just don't know. That was
his daddy talking on the phone. My son is gone. My baby
is dead. They're taking him away. Everything is gone.
Everything…

…She's as sweet, as Tupelo honey…

~ It's impossible… only a hunerd grams… That was
cousin Billy, still raving. … Wouldn't hurt a fuckin flea.

…Channel three news has confirmed that Elvis
Presley, the king of rock and roll, has died of
natural causes. Elvis Aron Presley, dead at
forty-two. Now this message…

~ Not my daddy…!

…Madge, look at my hands. They're not as
young as they used to be…

~ My son. My son.

Elvis sat in the attic, in the airless dark. Sweat poured
out of him, and streamed over him so fast it tickled and
made a puddle under his bare ass. He would just sit and
hum gospel tunes until somebody came and showed him
whichever way was home.

IT WAS LIKE A CIRCUS, but then a funeral always is. A dead person among the living, made up to look like the living, thaz like a circus trick. A big three-ring circus, a mob in front of shimmering Graceland, a long line snaking toward a polished copper coffin.

I hadn't thought about going to a funeral, and so I was wearing a dark sweater with my mother's embroidered scarf, way too hot for the sun beating down here in Memphis. Some of the crowd was dressed for Disneyland, torturing their children in strollers, and some were dressed for nightclubs. There were white women with their jewelry catching the sun over their freckled breasts, and black men wearing Sunday suits.

Jesse held my hand. He had a bad haircut, a crew cut that didn't suit him, but it was the best I could give him with the scissors I had borrowed at the motel. He had a bruise swelling up under his eye. Out in the bright sun I could see some flecks of gray paint that I hadn't scrubbed out. It had happened just up there, upstairs behind the bricks and columns, between those high windows. Strange, like a lifetime ago.

People said what people will say.

~ Minds me of when he was younger.

~ Must a been suffrin a lot... Took quite a toll on him...

~ Just good that his mama is already gone... Still a young woman, she woulda been...

~ ...Up there waitin for im.

A microphone whined. The singers were getting ready.

~ Is that JD, the bass man? That tall guy?

~ ...There's his daddy, see him? Not as old as I woulda thought.

~ ...That's him, you can hear him sobbing. Lord.

~ ...Who's that with him, is that her?

~ ...Lord, to lose a son... But he still got plenty a money...

~ ...Maybe she'll get it all... And the baby... set for life...

I didn't know I was going to get emotional. When we came near the foot of the coffin the smell of the flowers overpowered me. ~ God. This humidity. No wind or nothin. Make me appreciate the desert.

Jesse nodded. I rested my hand on the warm shiny edge of the coffin, which was covered with the smudges of people's palms and fingers. I wondered if they ever dug up the body, would they find my fingerprints there?

The nose was too narrow. The face was powdered and dry, dry as a doll's face. It was kind of wide, like Elvis's face, kind of puffy. Sam had done something clever with the lip. But the hair was wilting.

~ Don't look nothing like him, I whispered. Must've cut the sideburns from an old picture.

Jesse held on tight to my hand with both his hands. ~ Breathe baby, I said. He wanted to cry.

With my free hand I touched the rings on the man's hands. ~ I wonder, does your mother know where you are? I had to talk to him. Look at your face, and your hands with all the rings, but I don't even know who you are. Does anybody have the faintest idea? You were a sweet lil boy I bet, somebody's hope, somebody's pride and joy.

A big sob rose up out of Jesse.

~ What'd you do to get yourself here? You been in some prison all these years?

~ Mam? said the guard.

~ …You don't even know what a help you been. You saved a precious life.

~ Amen, someone said. All around folks had stopped their whispering and were dabbing their eyes, hearing the sweaty black woman, crazy with sudden grief, pouring out her heart.

~ …Here you are, and Elvis is on a bus headin for a better place. I jes hope for you that someone loves you an will never forget you.

~ Mam? The policeman put his white-gloved hand on my trembling shoulder. Mam, that was beautiful, but we got to keep moving.

Elvis hummed over the sizzle, throwing onions on the grill and laying on the salt and pepper.

Jesse took orders at the window. ~ You got it, Cindy. How bout you Tommy? Double chili and frazz. Double frazz. Sumpin to drink with that? Graveyard? Why not? Live a little.

~ Now Jess?

Jesse cocked his ear, sniffed once and nodded. Elvis flipped the burgers.

~ Graveyard beer, Zhoni. You know how Tommy likes em?

~ Root beer with choclit and cherry, dash of malt.

~ Right on. Got yours, Boss?

~ Got it. Elvis plopped on two more patties and hovered over the heat, spatula in hand.

Milly took a late break and sat at a table by the counter. She opened the newspaper to the middle, folded it and smoothed it out. ~ Here it is, she said through the layers of noise. Picture of the coffin. Can't see much. Face is all grainy. You shoulda been there, Boss.

~ Yep, like Huck Finn going to his own funeral. I'm outa salt, where's the...

~ Here it is, listen to this. Elvis Dee-En-Ay a Match. Dateline Mempfis Tinnesee. Dee-in-ay samples taken from the body of the diseased... de-ceased king of rock and roll last Tuesday show ay forty-nine-point-nine procent match with dee-in-ay taken from the father, Vernon Prezley. Both samples were drawn at Graceland mansion Augus six-teen, the day of the singer's death. This result was announced by the Shilby County Medical Egzaminer. A second, independent egzamination, conducted at the espress request of the Enquirerer, confirmed this conclusion. The dee-en-ay test, which regjisters a pattern of genetic information taken from the subject's blood, has a probable... ility of error of less than one in one... three, six... million.

~ Hold on Meem. Two the works Boss. Salt's down by your knee, see it? Show him, Nizhoni.

A fresh sizzle of grease. ~ Two cows, pink and brown. Turn the radio down? Okay Meem.

~ ...The dee-en-ay test is conclusive, according to Enquirerer reporter Kathy Kelly. It puts to rest perzistent rumors that the recent events at Graceland were an e-laborate hoax.

A beater whirred, then two beaters. Milly waited. ~ Three top, Carly.

~ ...Elaborate hoax... The enormously popular singer and actor was found nude... thaz what it says... on the floor of a bathroom in his twenny-one-room mansion last Tuesday. Elvis was overweight, said William Smith, a cousin and close friend of Prezley's. He was depressed. But none of us thought this could happen.

~ Thank you Billy.

~ ...Prezley's career had been in a steep decline.

Severe respire-ratory distress and cardiac aha-rhythm-ia were given as proximate causes of death. Drug abuse has not been ruled out.

~ Sounds serious, said Elvis.

Milly turned the paper over. ~ Here's another story. Po-lice Turn Out for Elvis. A motorcade of sevendy policemen, including thirdy motorcycles, led the funeral procession from Graceland to Forest Hills Cimetery. Prezley's involvement with law inforcement goes back to ay ninetteen-sevendy-one meeting with President Richard Nixon. He is reputed to have donated money and other aid to police departments in Mempfis Tinnesee and Laz Vegas Nevada.

Elvis flipped the burgers. ~ I wish I had my hog now. Wonder who's got it.

~ Why don't you buy one?

~ Where'm'I gonna get the cash?

~ Lord. Milly laid the paper down. You mean you...?

Elvis wrapped up the burgers. ~ We didn't exactly do that much estate planning. Anyway, when you start over you start over. I was choking on all that dough.

~ Wrap em tighter Boss.

~ Okay Jess. I'll practice. He flexed his fingers, ringless except for a plastic one on the pinky.

~ No cars. Take a break.

Elvis nodded and stretched and went around the counter. He paid attention to his walk, feeling out his balance, like a person coming home from a hospital. He loosened his apron and sat down with Milly.

She put her hand on his. ~ I could get the Cadillac back from ma.

He squirmed, embarrassed. ~ No. Thas all water under the bridge. I see all these kids coming in here… An my point is, how many times did my daddy and mama start over. Know what daddy did when he hit about the same age as me now? Picked up and left Tupelo where all the folks was an lit out for Memphis. With about enough money for gas an no job. Lookit me, I got a job. And when mama was about my age…

~ Well listen Elv… I mean Boss. We making money here. You'd be suprized.

~ Well I thought it all through, up there in that attic. Daddy got a couple hunerd mill. He's better off now that I'm gone. Cause if I'd've lived, the damn colonel would've….

~ Don't say that about your daddy, Elvis. He loves you.

~ I know baby, I didn't mean it that way. An Cilla got enough cash to spoil Lisa Marie half to death. That's all I care about. An gramma too. The rest of em can take a long walk.

~ What about that girl that was… that Ginger hussy.

Elvis fussed with his fingers where the rings used to be. ~ I don' even think about her.

~ Be honest now. Milly laced her fingers with his.

~Zhone, got some ones?

~All right I miss the sex a little.

Milly made a face.

Carly stopped near their table and looked over her shoulder and arched her back, checking her reflection in the darkening window.

~All right I just miss sex.

~You gon get that back baby. Look at your hand. See, you were all swoll up before. It's already going down.

Elvis looked at his hands, spreading his fingers and turning them back and forth. He fidgeted in his chair.

~You still got this plasticky one. That from your baby girl?

~Yuh.

~We'll get you some more rings baby. You want something blue, like this one?

~That looks nice on you.

Milly's earrings bobbed. The compliment actually made her blush.

Carly went out the door, then peeked back in. ~One car. Single.

Milly stood up.

~You know, said Elvis, there's one thing I'd still like to do.

~Whaz that, doll baby. She stood behind him and adjusted his hamburger man hat.

~I'm turning the sign, said Nizhoni. Okay? She jiggled her necklaces in the glass, and turned the black CLOSED to the red OPEN side.

~ I want to walk on the beach.

~ Ain't got no beaches roun here.

~ You know I spent all those days and nights in Honalulu, and I never had time to walk on the beach. Well, never took time. Never even took my shoes off. Cept when the camera was rollin.

~ We can save up, said Milly.

Carly came to the table and emptied her apron, coins dapping on the plastic tablecloth. Milly, sighing, had a few to add, and Nizhoni came over too and brought some handfulls out of her apron.

~ Six, seven… ten, eleven, eleven-fifty… elevenfifty-eight?

~ We're going to split it three ways, Boss.

~ We decided. We're going to cut you in till you get your first paycheck.

~ One, two, three… and this goes back in the kitty.

Carly pushed the change into the coffee can. Nizhoni picked up one of the little clinking piles and put it in Elvis's hand. ~ How you gonna spend it?

~ Oh, I guess I'll get a doll for my little girl.

~ I'll make one for you.

~ With a little blanket?

~ Sure.

~ You're a nice guy, Boss. Help us clean up?

Milly looked seriously at Elvis and said, ~ How you gonna send stuff to your little girl?

~You can send it to her. She knows you.

A dime rolled into the juke box.

Jesse came to the counter wiping his hands on his apron. ~You two gonna set here all night?

Milly folded her arms. ~Maybe.

…Nnow it begins, llet it begi-i-ahin…

Clean-up ti-i-ime!

Milly and the girls put together a home movie, starting with Elvis squinting at a headline – Elvis Kidnapped by Space Aliens, Due Back in 1987. He sweeps up the Burger Joint, he tries to touch his toes. He blows a kiss and says Hi mama, I love you. It shows a hurting, shaken Elvis talking on the phone with his daddy and with his grandma during their illnesses. Milly, slimmer and camera shy, holds his hand. There is a sweet sequence where he wraps presents with the girls, and one where he careens around the Joint on his bicycle. He looks proud showing off his AA badge, seven years clean and sober. Then there they are at the rim of the Grand Canyon, a little over-exposed, and Elvis pretends to jump off. Nizhoni, now a big woman with kids, trims his hair. In a paper hat and tee-shirt he demonstrates his burger-flipping technique, and the camera pans to an article taped above the grill that says Elvis Lives, Flips Burgers, next to a Hawaii travel poster.

♛

~ Mahalo everybody… My name is Lani Kamakawiwo'ole, you probly hear me on my show on K-HON. Maybe you don' know what size I am. The bright Pacific breeze rustled her wavy hair and her sumptuous leis and scudded in her microphone. On stage here tonight we're going to have big little brudda Izz an a Haole band. But righ now we're going to have the first annual, we hope okay? Elvis imitation contest, and right out here is the dock where Elvis chased down the crooks on the speedboat. Too big of waves today, they would have to wait a while. But here on shore, everything fine, no problem.

She paused and looked around at the people smiling back at her radiant smile. ~ Pau hana, okay? everybody just have fun. Our first contestant is from over on a Big Island and his name is Glen Yamauchi.

Glen took the mike in both hands and bowed. The music started and he swiveled his hips. …Awella blussa ma soula wasa wroang with me…

In their seats over to the side Milly was talking. ~ Jeezuz that gal's big. Make me feel skinny.

~ You're jus right honey, said Elvis. Jesse kept his eyes on the stage.

~ That guy's terrible, said Milly.

~ I don' know. His voice is kind of fresh. Like mine used to be.

~ How's my hair?

~Wind blown.

> …Ahm in love. Ahm all shook up… mm-mm-
> mm…

~You think they got an extra jack? said Elvis

~I doubt it, said Jesse. This whole thing is kinda thrown together.

~Well listen then let's skip the guitar part. So Milly, on the second number you can add a little up top, all right?

~No baby I aint addin nothin. Jus what we practiced.

~But remember I showed you…

~Jesse got that. Don'cha Jesse?

> …Mm-mm-mmm, h-mm hyeah-yeah, ahm all
> shook up.

~Let's hear it for this Big Island Elvis.

The applause was enthusiastic. Lani stopped the happy singer and put a lei around his neck to another flurry of applause.

~Our next contestants tole me, they are fifty-one years old, fifty-two? a same age that Elvis would be. And also, they were born in Meess-iz-sippi in a same town as Elvis. Meess-iz-sippi reevah, shinin like a nachunal guit-tah… An they're going to play a piano and sing a medally. So please welcome, all a way from Phoenix on a mainland, mister Jesse Martin and the New All-Night Singers!

tluntluntlun tuntn…. runtuntuhnta tuhn and all three came right in, ~Aamayyy-zi-i-ing grace, ohhow sweet thuh-uh so-o-ouund… Milly high and wavery, Elvis down low in a dark groove, Jesse zig-zagging between…. Tha-ad sa-eyved a-a-a rrwretch, laahh-hik meee. Elvis added a *toon-tn-tn-toon* like a string base on the low keys. The mike wasn't getting all of this, but there was a sweet zone around Jesse. Lani felt it…. A-nd grayce wihill lead, meeyee hhome… he told her.

The applause wasn't very loud, the way their little church at home might sound without the church walls. The wind swept across the stage and fluttered Lani's skirt. Lani laughed with the crowd and said, ~ I loved that! So authentic. Her mike caught the roar of the wind, and she turned sideways to shelter it. ~ We migh have to wait for the wind to die down a little. Righ now I would like to give a big mahalo to Davy our soun man. He has a biiig job today. The sound man shrugged under his straw hat and tried moving some more switches.

And I would like to give a big thank you to our sponsors, Fernandez Chevrolet and Cadillac, sponsor of the whole Blue Hawaii festival, and it's going on all weekend. So give them some applause okay? The warm Hawaii kine.

And, also, the people here from Matsui Shave Ice with the real down homay Hawaii flavors on a North Shore. They got a stan righ down over there. I like a Blue Hawaii coco-nut. That's my favorite kine.

Okay we say aloha and mahalo to the wind god, and better say aloha to Pe-le too. The New All-Night Singers have another song and this is Boss Smith, that's your real name right? And he is Jesse's little brudda. Welcome all the way to Hawaii Boss, and the reason he is not all dressed up is, he is the way Elvis would be today if he had not have passed away, ten years ago already, I can't believe it. So here Elvis you can come up to the mike and tell us about it.

~Thank you. Thank you very much. It's nice to be back here, back here in Hawaii. He sheltered the mike from the wind with his hand, and if you were looking you could see a dimple on his cheek that would remind you of Elvis. I jus love that sand under my feet. I'd like to try livin here some day.

Lani smiled big and applauded and a few joined her in the bemused audience.

~Well it's a long story how I got here. Uh the short version is, uh the life I was living was killing me. An then when I was dyin a hand jus reached down and...

~Amen, somebody said. The crowd was trying to stay with him. He laughed, just a natural laugh. Anybody who had known him way back when would recognize him now.

He looked at his hand, the one with the turquoise and the hammered silver band and the plastic pinky ring. ~Ah, where was I? Oh yeah. Anyway, he pulled me up outa there. Gimme an E chord Jess. We are, climbin, Jacob's, ladder, we are, climbin, Jacob's ladder... The piano finished the thought and Elvis was saying, One of the mistakes I made, one of the many, uh, was, uh, I let other people tell me what I could sing. Well excep gospel, I always stayed with that.

Hwhen I'm growing old an feeb-lle, stand by me.

~ Staand byy mee, Jesse and Milly answered and spread out some lavender chords and Elvis gave the mike cord a little flip and cleared his throat.

~ Here's a song I coulda sung if I'd a had the God-given sense to be my own man.

~ Amen, from the crowd. Yes Lord.

~ Okay brutha, let's do it. *Ba da dunt dun. Ba da dunt dun…* The piano set down the base line.

~ And this is how I sing it now, *ba da da dunt dun*, because the truth is… Elvis lives.

The curious crowd forgot the sandals and slacks and off-the-rack island shirt and the string necklace and ignored the shiny bare spots the wind made in his hair and cheered for Elvis lives.

~ And so do you Jesus brutha, when the night, has come, ohoh an the land, is dark. and the moo-oon, is the only, light I see. Cuz that's the way we started so why should I be, afrai-id? no-o I won't be afraid, cuz I been dead already, As long, as you stan, stan by me. Sing it with me darlin darlin stan by me, o-o-o-oh stan, by me, oh sta-an…

The audience finished it for him and the mike swooshed in the wind. ~ Because you know the sky, did fall, yes the sky did fall, and y'know the mountain did crumble, to the sea. An I cried, yes I did cry, for my baby I cry every day, but I'm still here cuz you stan, stan by me, darlin darlin stan… Moving his-sort-of-in-shape body to the clean rhythm, he reminded people of the fresh innocent rebel and made them feel good.

~Hey, you pretty good, said Lani. Let's have a big hand for Boss Smith an Elvis lives. The clapping was appreciative, with a couple of light-hearted whoops. Elvis and Jesse stood side by side, one relaxed, the other suddenly anxious, facing all these people he didn't know. Elvis put his hand on his brother's back, but Lani's arm with her pile of bracelets was already there. ~They like you guys. They're still clapping.

Lani lifted one of her leis over her head, bowed her head and waited for Jesse to do the same, and laid the flowers tenderly around his neck. She arranged the lei on his shoulders. Is she your wife?

~She's my auntie.

~What, your auntie? Wow, you don't look old enough.

~I'm not, said Milly, receiving her flowers. Oooh these are nice. You aint his type by the way.

~Is this your boyfriend? Lani raised another lei for Elvis.

Lani said, ~Stick around, okay? Jesse looked to see who she was talking to and looked right into her sunny brown eyes.

He was still walking off stage in a dazzle of sunlight when the speakers began to thump. A young man in a red spangled jump suit stood twitching next to the stage.

~Our next Elvis comes to us all a way from a bright

lights of Las Vegas. Please give up a biiig welcome to Elvis' little brother, King Sonny Park!

King Sonny leapt onto the stage, took the mike with ringed hands and paced like a caged panther as far as the cord would allow.

Well its a one fo the money…

two fo the show…

threeda get ready now go cat go…

He was already sweating. The audience got out of their chairs and crowded up against the stage.

~ Mail man's here. Make him a cherry coke, Boss?

~ You got it Latoka. Any more cars?

~ Nope.

Elvis swirled in the cherry syrup and handed it to Latokadust and she handed him the mail. He leafed through it. ~ Seventeen, did you have dibs on this? Bill, bill, ad, hey here's a postcard.

He came around the counter, to where teenage Choya was standing on a chair, helping decorate the Burger Joint for a dance. Milly was taking a paper chain from a big cardboard box and handing it up, and Victory was there too, hanging around waiting for Carly to get off work.

~ Hey, I got a post card here. From Jesse. Elvis showed them the card, a brown hula girl in a grass skirt and flower lei.

~What's it say, Boss?

He fished the glasses out of his apron pocket. ~ Dear Milly and Boss and everybody... Mahalo! Wish you were here.

~Yeah sure. The boy jumped down from the chair to read over his shoulder.

~I have been learning to hula, can you believe it? We have been walking on the beach too and Lani's bra...

~Bro, said the boy. Like brother.

~...Bra, bro, is trying to teach me how to surf.

Carly, coming in the door, ran right into Victory. ~ Dang! He stood there looking at his spilled soda.

~Well, you shouldn't stand in front of the door like that, Vic.

~Leave it, said Elvis. I got it. He handed the card to Choya and went around the counter.

~There's a Cadillac outside, said Carly. Brand new. Got kind of a crooked license plate.

Victory picked up his paper cup and peered out. ~Looks like a big green hearse. Chick getting out. Foxy.

~We got a post card from Jesse. He's surfin and everything.

~Let's see.

~She says aloha to everybody. Must be that Lani.

~Doesn't that mean good-bye?

~It's backwards for hello.

~It means love too.

Outside, the young woman walked through the heat

and stopped at the door. She took off her sunglasses and held them tightly. She came in. She was wearing slacks and sandals and a blue vee-neck sweater with a glass bead necklace. She was maybe twenty and her face was good-looking but kind of sharp like she had already lived a lot. She stood looking at Milly like she was seeing a ghost.

~ Is my daddy here?

Elvis came around the counter, humming, pushing a mop bucket in front of him. He looked up and saw the young woman, and the pain and hope in her face.

Playlist

Mahalia Jackson – "His Eye is on the Sparrow" (Civilla Martin & Charles Gabriel)
Alan Dale – "Cherry Pink and Apple Blossom White" (Perez Prado)
Elvis Presley – "That's All Right Mama" (Arthur Crudup)
Gene Krupa, Arthur Crudup

Elvis Presley – "It's Now or Never" (Shroeder & Gold) from "O Solo Mio" (Giovanni Capurros & Eduardo di Capua), "Return to Sender" (Otis Blackwell & Winfield Scott)
Ray Price, BB King, Jimi Hendrix, Janis Joplin, Aretha Franklin, Carl Perkins, Willa Mae Thornton, Junior Parker
Sun Records, Memphis, founded by Sam Phillips
Elvis Presley with the Jordanaires – "Teddy Bear" (Kal Mann & Bernie Lowe)
Ray Charles

The Stamps, 1977: JD Sumner, Ed Hill, Ed Enoch & Bill Baize
Elvis Presley – "He Touched Me" (William J Gaither)
The Sweet Inspirations, 1977: Sylvia Shemwell, Myrna Smith & Estelle Brown
Elvis Presley – "Put Your Hand in the Hand of the Man" (Gene MacLellan), "Swing Down Chariot" (Negro Spiritual), "Lead Me, Guide Me" (Doris Akers), "All My Trials" (Caribbean Negro Spiritual)
Rod Stewart – "Tonight's the Night"
Elvis Presley – "I Believe" (Drake, Graham, Shirl & Stillman), "Heartbreak Hotel" (Mae Boren Axton, Durden, Presley)
Ben E. King – "Spanish Harlem" (Lieber & Stoller)
King Curtis
Aretha Franklin – "Spanish Harlem" (Lieber & Stoller)
Jerry Lieber & Mike Stoller, Ronnie Spector, Diana Ross
Johnny Rivers – "Secret Agent Man" (PF Sloan & Steve Barri)
Elvis Presley – "My Happiness" (Betty Peterson Blasco & Barney Bergantine)

Elvis Presley – "In the Ghetto" (Mac Davis), "Can't Help Falling in Love" (Peretti, Creatore & Weiss), "Wooden Heart" (Fred Wise, Bert Kaemfert & Kay Twomey), from "Muss I Denn" (a German folk song preserved by PF Silcher)

Speech by Adolf Hitler

Movies "Born to Run" & "Blue Hawaii"

Tuesday Weld, Ann Margret

Elvis Presley in a Las Vegas concert

Dion – "Abraham, Martin & John" (Dick Holler)

BB King playing Lucille, his guitar

Al Stewart – "The Year of the Cat" (Al Stewart & Peter Wood)

Television show "As the World Turns," commercial for a Proctor and Gamble product

Thelma Houston – "Don't Leave Me This Way" (Ken Gamble, Leon Hall & Cary Gibbons)

Junior Parker – "Mystery Train" (Herman Parker Jr & Sam Phillips)

Radio station WDIA, Memphis

Elvis Presley – "Peace in the Valley" (Thomas A Dorsey)

Gilbert O'Sullivan – "Alone Again Naturally"

Marvin Gaye, "What's Going On" (Al Cleveland, Marvin Gaye, Renaldo Benson)

Van Morrison – "Tupelo Honey"

J.D. Sumner, Israel Kamakawiwo'ole

John Lennon & Yoko Ono – "Cleanup Time"

Elvis Presley – "All Shook Up" (Otis Blackwell), "Amazing Grace" (John Newton & William Walker)

Paul Simon – "Graceland"

"Jacob's Ladder" (Negro Spiritual), "Stand By Me" (Charles A Tindley), "Stand By Me" (Lieber & Stoller)

Elvis Presley – "Blue Suede Shoes" (Carl Perkins)

Thanks to Kathleen LaMear, Marie, Molly & Philip McCarty, Vesta Eaton, and my whole family, Desmond O'Grady, Kikumi Islam, Michael Smith, John Labovitz, Patti Battin, Kim Kacalek, Jim O'Neal of the Delta Blues Museum, all my friends and most especially Kelley Morehouse.